Also by Dathan Belanger

The Faith of a Centurion

Clean Forgotten Patriots:
In the American War of Independence

Angels and Miracles on the Battlefield

Rise of the Reprobi: Book One: The First Revolution Series

Published by Clay Bridges in Houston, TX
www.claybridgespress.com

eISBN: 978-1-68488-026-3
Pb- ISBN: 978-1-68488-027-0
Hb- ISBN: 978-1-68488-028-7

Special Sales: Clay Bridges titles are available in wholesale quantity. Please visit www.claybridgesbulk.com to order 10 or more copies at a retail discount. Custom imprinting or excerpting can also be done to fit special needs. Contact Clay Bridges at Info@ClayBridgesPress.com.

RISE OF THE
REPROBI

— Book One: The First Revolution Series —

Dathan Belanger

CLAY BRIDGES
P R E S S

*A special thanks to Dylan Baranski
for helping bring the Reprobi voices to life.*

TABLE OF CONTENTS

TABLE OF CONTENTS

PREFACE

I enjoy writing Historical Fiction. My desire is to immerse readers in an interesting and important epoch of history to entertain them and, perhaps, teach them a lesson or two. Because I agree with philosopher George Santayana's famous quote, "Those who do not learn history are doomed to repeat it." If we fail to remember our history and learn its lessons, we are squandering a wealth of knowledge.

This book is a bit of a new wrinkle for me, as it is a work of *Alternative* Historical Fiction. In my previous books, *The Faith of a Centurion*, *Clean Forgotten Patriots: In the American War of Independence*, and *Angels and Miracles on the Battlefield*, I placed my characters in historical events as they actually played out.

On the other hand, *The Rise of the Reprobi*, asks the question, "What if?" Specifically, "What if Lucifer had been let out of hell at the turning point of the American Revolutionary War? What if the Americans, with quintessential characters like George Washington and Alexander Hamilton, as well as British and Native Americans, had been forced to deal with him? What would that have looked like?" *The Rise of the Reprobi* is my answer. This story will appeal to history buffs and fantasy fiction fans alike. More importantly, readers will come away with a better understanding of the line between good and evil and with a greater appreciation of that which is true power.

I hope you enjoy it—and learn a bit.

—Dathan

INTRODUCTION

The American Revolution was at its most desperate time to survive. The British now controlled New York City and the strategic Fort Ticonderoga in upstate New York, and they were making an advance on Philadelphia. Their objective was to capture the rebel capital and end the war. They loaded 15,000 British Regulars and Hessian troops on an armada of ships and sailed from New York City to the Chesapeake Bay in Maryland. Next, the army advanced north to capture Philadelphia. On September 11th, General George Washington attempted to block them along the banks of the Brandywine River in Pennsylvania but was given a crushing defeat.

After the Battle of Brandywine, Washington kept his army in Pennsylvania between Philadelphia and Reading to keep an eye on the British and to protect important military supplies recently moved out of the Philadelphia area to Reading. He gave orders to General Wayne—known as "Mad" Anthony Wayne—to harass the British at every chance with but a modest force. Wayne made the serious mistake of thinking his camp was well-hidden. On September 20, 1777, at 10 PM, British troops attacked the camp. In a surprise attack, they charged into the camp with fixed bayonets. In what became known as the Paoli Massacre, Wayne fled in panic as the British poured into camp. His entire force was routed with most of them captured.

Washington desperately wanted to prevent British forces from taking Philadelphia, but a thousand of his men were barefoot and his army was exhausted from hard marches under heavy rains, from fording rivers, and often going without food. On September 26, Philadelphia, America's largest city, was captured by the British, and Congress, which had met there, fled. Pennsylvanians lowered the Liberty Bell and carted it to the basement of the Zion Reformed Church in Allentown, where they hid it.

The politicians in Congress, who had no understanding of military operations, were now safely in York, Pennsylvania. They urged Washington to take up the offensive and attack the British in Philadelphia, but the commander-in-chief was not a fool. His men were exhausted and supplies were low. His soldiers wore tattered uniforms and many were barefoot. He decided it was best to look for a location for the army's winter encampment. Washington sought the advice of his generals, but they were unable to come to a conclusion. Finally, he decided the matter alone. On December 12th, the army began a miserable 13-mile march to the west bank of the Schuylkill River at Valley Forge.

During this time, a tremor stirred in the bowels of the earth. A hot magma bulge deep beneath New England's surface shifted. It affected part of the tectonic plate that had up until then only moved consistently 1.48 inches annually, the same rate the moon spins away from the earth or about the same rate our fingernails grow. A barely detectable earthquake awoke through the earth's crust and broke what had never been broken before. A powerful seal that had been in place to keep out "The First Revolution."

Perhaps whoever placed the seal knew this day would come. Perhaps it was a preordained time, though the inhabitants below the barrier would be an evil threat to those above it. It is said that all sin can be redeemed through the grace of God. Was this an opportunity for redemption? A chance out of their prison to rejoin the blessed. Unfortunately for the earth, the dwellers below had free will. It is said free will can be a blessing and a curse. Alas, in this case, it was a curse.

CHAPTER 1

LUCIFER'S DREAM

The only word that could ever describe the setting is "paradise." The sun shone brilliantly, bathing the lush green canopy. The air was a perfect 70 degrees without a hint of humidity. It was a splendid and bountiful utopia. Beautiful flora, both colorful and vivid, gave off a heavenly scent in the air. The brilliant blue water was interwoven through the landscape as gentle rivers and breathtaking waterfalls. Among the flourishing vegetation was a countless variety of vegetable plants and fruit trees in every size, shape, and color—imagined and unimagined. The Garden of God—known to man as the Garden of Eden—was created to be paradise on earth and it delivered exactly that.

A perfect, angelic being walked confidently through the lush green grass in this heavenly paradise. The angel wore not a shred of clothing, unashamed of his nakedness. The only adornment was a simple gold wreath on his head. In a leisurely stroll, the angel walked up a tall hill and stopped. The top of the hill revealed two enormous trees in full bloom. Petals glided gently down.

A voice boomed from above. "Lucifer, of you I am most proud. The ripples you make will echo through eternity."

Lucifer grinned as he looked up. "Lord, you are joyful. Please show yourself to me?"

An impossible bright light made from pure energy appeared from the sky. Only the blessed could see it without becoming instantly blind.

Lucifer continued, "Lord, your humble servant who loves you asks you to allow him to rule over your new creation, Man. This will allow you more time to create. More time to love. I am not alone in my request." Up the hill marched an entire Legion of angels. Six thousand, six hundred, and sixty-six to be precise in perfect nude form. "My friends that love me, and I, them, support my claim. You are proud and pleased with me. I beg of you to grant your most loyal servant this request."

A thunderous voice. "My answer is no. I am the I am that has ruled the heavens since eternity with the power of love that lies within me. You do not see in your heart that this request is out of pride and not out of love for me."

A thin dark beam appeared to strike the light in a battle for supremacy. The fight was short-lived. The blackness vanished till only the light remained. Lucifer hung his shoulders in defeat. His body was lifted into the air. With a grimace, his body began to contort from a feeling never felt before. Pain. His wreath went through his head and formed two golden horns resembling that of a goat. His skin began to bubble till it took on the appearance of a red snake. His hands and feet turned into a reptilian form with large claws. He dropped from the air landing on his feet. As the pain began to dull, he looked over his new appearance. He screamed with his whole body. His eyes were wide with terror, mouth agape, claws digging deep into the palms of his hand as he clenched his fists.

The entire Legion of his followers transformed into similar creatures. The only exception was that Lucifer had his horns. The horns serve as his crown. The transformed Legion began to blink out one by one until only Lucifer remained.

A voice blared from on high, "I am displeased with your display of pride, you know the lessons of love that I have taught and that I have shown to you. You will not rule men. You will rule as the prince of darkness. Because I love you, I will not destroy you. I cast you out of heaven to think of your folly and come back to love."

A single tear rolled down Lucifer's face.

Lucifer awoke. He was sitting on his throne made from chiseled stone. The darkened cavern that held his throne was cut from the same stone. Moisture from the humidity of the cavern sweated down the ceiling and walls and over time formed into shallow pools on the floor. In the silence, you could hear the water collect in them. No movement of air, only a stagnated musty and earthy smell.

As the prince of darkness, he held no luxury other than a simple black linen robe. He still preferred to be nude but a chill in the air kept him from it. The fallen angels called Reprobi were not deep enough to benefit from thermal heat. The pride in his heart was still warm over the centuries, but never enough to warm his bones. Hell was a rather cold place.

Lucivia approached. His reptilian skin was colored red and black. A perfect cross between a human and a mud snake.

"My Lord," Lucivia said, as he bowed his head in submission. "Although it feels like an eternity, the invisible field we could not pass has weakened somehow in a random location. A crack has been found. We were able to exploit it. We have reached the surface." A twisted grin came on his face. "I personally led a recon a few miles outside the entrance. The earth is in the season of winter. The wintry conditions up there wreak havoc on our cold blood. Alcohol spirits derived from decaying vegetation will give us a lift but we have unfortunately a limited supply. We may have to wait for warmer weather to further explore."

Lucifer's eyes glowed red as he listened to everything Lucivia had to say. When Lucivia was finished speaking. A flash of euphoria lit his face. "Tell Rexus to gather the Legion at once. I wish to address them."

"Yes, my Lord." Lucivia bowed again then ran.

Lucifer pondered with his only true friend: himself. *Why is the seal open now? The only time I was ever allowed release was to tempt Jesus. Is this crack in the seal on purpose? The father never said he would punish me for eternity. Am I being freed and changed back to my original form? Is this a test? Should I come back freely to the light?*

His face contorted in anger. "No! We shall take what should have been ours and we will rule this world!"

Shortly afterward, Rexus—Lucifer's second-in-command—entered. Though similar in his snake-like appearance as Lucifer's other minions, Rexus could be distinguished by his jet-black skin of a king cobra, with a hood created by elongated ribs that extended from the lower skin on his neck outwards. His robe was dark grey in color.

Rexus bowed before Lucifer. "My Lord," Rexus said.

"At ease, my friend."

Rexus stood up.

"Rexus, do you know why I have summoned you here?"

"No, my Lord."

"For an unexplained reason, an open fissure has been found in the seal that has damned us to this underworld for eons. Rather than waste valuable time questioning why it has appeared, I have decided to take advantage of it in case this is temporary. Therefore, I want you to gather up half of the Legion, 3,333, and exit our hole. Our brotherhood has work to do. Work that is long overdue."

Rexus raised an eyebrow. "Are you suggesting that . . . ?"

"Yes, I am. We're going to conquer and enslave all of mankind as it was always meant to be."

"But what if God detects our actions? We'll be stopped for certain!"

Lucifer smirked. "He won't.

"I ask with deep respect; how do you know?"

"Because God knows everything. Always omnipresent with the holy spirit to do his bidding. He has allowed this to happen. He wants us to rule over man. Now enough banter; I want my order carried out immediately. We have waited long enough. It's time for the Reprobi to rise again"

Rexus nodded slightly. "I ssshall obey, although I must ask: where is this fissure?"

"Lucivia will guide you to it. It opens to an area the humans call Valley Forge. It shan't be too hard to find."

"It will be as you command," Rexus hissed.

Rexus marched off to make his preparations with half the Legion strength as Lucifer commanded. Though the future hadn't been written in stone, Lucifer had trouble stifling an evil laugh as he relished the thought of subjugating everyone on earth.

The entire Legion gathered in a cavern that wormed its way deep into the earth. The cavern was cut during the last ice age. The walls above arched a hundred feet up to giant stalactites formed from thick mineral deposits dripping from above the cavern.

Lucifer stood with Rexus by his side.

Lucifer addressed the Reprobi, "We have been cursed to suffer you and me, but the suffering has now come to an end. Together we will conquer the world that should have been ours to rule from the beginning. We will make ourselves lords over the men of this planet. Half of you will go forth with Rexus to bleed them. We rape, pillage, and bring fear to their hearts. In time they will love only us instead of God. Sharpen your blades, my brothersss."

The assembly exploded with howls and cheers. All that waiting, all those long boring days, they never thought freedom was even possible, but it had come! The Reprobi believed it was all Lucifer's doing. They believed to their core that only Lucifer was the good shepherd to lead and guide them. Joining their voices together, they began to chant, "Lucifer! Lucifer!" to show their appreciation with every ounce of strength in their lungs.

Their banishment was long but had nothing on eternity. The fallen angels, the Reprobi, were ready to rise again.

CHAPTER 2

ASCENSION FROM HELL

It is said that if a tree falls and no one is there to hear it, a sound may still be made. There was no sound here. The deep forest held under an awning of bright fall colors was devoid of any sounds of life. Life, which had always been so abundant, vanished without a trace as if afraid to be heard. A large stone was rolled over. The dark earth beneath began to shake and rumble. A reptilian black arm slowly pushed its way out of the earth followed by a body. The Reprobi had ascended from the abyss of hell.

This Reprobi was named Luciviathanaton, or Lucivia for short. He stood seven feet tall and looked like a perfect cross of a man and a red and black mud snake, although the head with its bright yellow eyes was slightly more snake-like. His razor-sharp fangs and claws appeared menacing. Over his scaly skin, a sheen of oily film covered his entire body. It reeked of death and decay.

A thin black cloak produced from tiny threads found in insect cocoons beneath the earth was the only protection from the elements. Underneath the cloak, he wore the *lorica segmentata* armor that consisted of iron strips fastened to internal leather straps with shoulder guards. In the back were cut holes where two black stubs replaced once feathery wings.

Lucivia flittered his long, thin tongue—which had a forked part at the tip—back and forth, smelling the forest. An evil grin contorted his lips, and an unearthly cackle echoed through the forest.

Next out of the hole was Rexus. Lucivia lay himself before Rexus. It was not that he was a foot taller and visibly stronger, but it was Rexus that led the expedition. His command was given to him because of his blind obedience to the Prince of Darkness and his attention to detail. He was a vicious viper when assigned a task; no matter how small or large, it would always be completed thoroughly.

Rexus inhaled deeply, then visibly shook from the cold. "I can feel the wind on my face and it's marvelous. I've forgotten the sssensation, but I would rather feel the blood of man sprayed on it."

"I have not felt such joy in a long time," said Lucivia. "I want to run free and see everything, to see how much the earth has changed since creation."

"You will feel this joy soon, my brother. With eternity, the wait is but a blink of the eye. Lucifer will provide everlasting joy. Stay the course; you will have time to frolic later."

"Your words do not comfort me, but I obey the Prince of Darkness and I will do as you command."

"Indeed, you must. You're the best scout among us. We trust you to serve and obey."

Lucivia frowned. "We will need more supplies and equipment from below, especially spirit drinksss to deal with this cold."

"The remaining Reprobi will not be denied their share of supplies. We will make do with what we have. What is a little discomfort compared to eons of imprisonment we have just endured below the earth's crust?"

Lucivia tilted his head slightly. "As you command," he said flatly. "Though I shall admit, I disagree with your assessment."

Rexus gently caressed the pommel of his short sword. "You never have been one to accept things as they are, have you? Have faith in Lucifer. He will not fail us."

"Of course, my brother, I have faith in him. I would not be in this creature's form if it was not so."

The Reprobi ascended out of the hole, and one by one they prostrated themselves in front of Rexus as a sign of submission to their commander. After the final Reprobi emerged, they covered the hole and replaced the rock.

Besides claws sharpened until they were sharp enough to slice a man's throat with a light pass, they were equipped with battle axes, either single- or double-bladed, and sharp enough to cleave a head off in one blow; some wore a short sword called a *gladius*, designed to stick deep and with a twist pull out the guts of its victims; others brought and stacked *pilas*, heavy seven-foot-long javelins, each with a barbed tip designed to punch through an opponent's armor or shield and skewer him. For defense, each wore the lorica segmentata armor and held a heavy rectangular iron shield, heavy enough to be unwieldy for a man, but an easy lift for a Reprobi.

Rexus and Lucivia watched the army form into tight rows.

Rexus released an ugly roar that sounded like a breathy "uh," as though gasping for air.

"The first Revolution continuesss," bellowed Rexus. "We have been released from our prison to claim what is rightfully ours to rule. The humans are mere puppets that will dance before us." He raised his fist to the sky. "God has taken our wings, but we will get them back and return to our true forms. Beauty lost will be returned. Lucifer will lead us to victory and glory. He alone is the master of our salvation. He alone is the doer of right." He grabbed the standard and waved it viciously.

A thunderous sound of shouts and cheers erupted along with the banging of their weapons on their shields.

Rexus turned to Lucivia. "Scouts will have first dibs on our spirits. Take out your scouts and get closer to the humans. Gather as much intel as you can; I want to know my enemy. And keep stealth, we do not want them to notice us yet. Your scouts will be tempted to kill but they must stay their hands." A low growl. "Sssoon we will get our fill." Rexus looked directly into Lucivia's eyes. "Also, by any means necessary capture one of these humans and send them to me. I have many questions to ask."

Lucivia snapped his fist to his chest. "As you command. We will leave at once."

The Legion dispersed to set up camp. They used the surrounding forest to cut branches for shelters. They kept the shelters low and camouflaged them with the surrounding foliage.

By nightfall, they surrounded their campfires. They dug them deep under the ground to hide the flames and smoke from human eyes. Logs ablaze settled in the fire pits with loud cracks. They drew out wet stones and sharpened their offensive weapons, claws, and blades.

Rexus walked the campgrounds inspecting the work. A white fleck of snow drifted gently to land on the tip of his nostrils. He looked up and watched the flakes dance with the wind. He shifted his thin cloak tighter around himself and took a sip from his canteen. The foul-tasting spirits sent a warming sensation throughout his body starting from his core, and then through his limbs. The spirits were not needed to warm his mind. It was already ablaze with thought. This was the opportunity for the Reprobi to rise again. He would not fail his Lord.

CHAPTER 3

LEARNING CURVE

The sun's bright light brought out the purity of the white frost as if it were a blessed blanket. The creature standing on it was damned. The temperature continued to drop as the morning ended. He was nowhere near the coldest place on earth, but it was hell on earth for any who had never experienced winter before.

Rexus looked down at his clawed hand. He opened and closed his fist slowly. His exposed arms and legs felt a burning sensation he never felt before, not from heat, but from the cold, so cold it hurt. He felt a sensation of heaviness in his limbs as he labored toward a massive fire set deep in a hole in the ground. The tall flames licked the air, fighting back against mother nature's sting. His muscles barely registered. In fact, they were practically misfiring, but they began to stir slowly as he felt the warmth of the fire.

Atticus, second in charge of the Legion, prostrated himself before Rexus. His reptilian skin was marble-colored, grey, and light brown. A perfect cross between a human and a rattlesnake. He rose slowly.

"We are improving the shelter as you ordered," said Atticus. "We have dug deeper and reinforced the ceilings with timber. The fire pits are deeper now and the smoke is properly vented."

Rexus smacked his palm with the bottom of his fist. "Curse this reptilian blood mix! It mocks us, oh, it mocks us. From the dawn of our creation, we have never felt such . . . such misery!"

"Perhaps so, but I do have a favorite thing about this weather . . ."

Rexus hissed angrily. "And *what* is that!?"

"When it's over," said Atticus.

Rexus shot a blank stare at Atticus. It was obvious Rexus didn't get the quip.

Atticus cast his glare around, looking for a way to change the subject. "Food is still an issue. If we do not venture out further to collect it, we will be in trouble. I know we will not starve, but the energy reduction . . . well it can reduce us to a pitiful state even worse than this wretched weather."

"Send a few back to Lucifer to grab more from the stores and send my reports to him," Rexus said. "There will be more roots for now, but fresh meat will be soon on the menu."

"What are your orders for the Legion?"

"The camp guard remains for any uninvited guestsss. We remain here and we continue to stay hidden. No word will be spoken, not a sound without my say so. I will allow one centurion at a time to come out to drill his Legionaries. They need to get used to moving on the surface.

"We can't do much in this weather, it's a curse upon us."

"Patience, yes, patience. This weather will turn, I am sure of it."

Atticus cast a quizzical look with his eyes.

"It is the planet that is cursed," Rexus said. "You forget this planet revolves around a star referred to as the 'sun'. Its elongated orbit and tilt . . . oh, never mind. Know that Lucifer would have made a better design if he was given the opportunity to create."

"Maybe there's a reason for the design?"

Rexus' eyes gave off heat. "Go!"

Atticus walked away and as the heat of the fire dissipated, he moved like one in a scene out of a slow-motion projector.

Rexus watched the first of thirty centuries under his command deploy in a practice drill. Each century had an average of 100 Legionnaires. Each Legionnaire was given one heavy swallow of spirits before they began. The first formation was the tortoise formation. The defensive formation was so strong that it doubled as a bridge that they used as a portable step ladder so that their comrades could stand on it to climb over low walls and throw javelins. The Reprobi in the front ranks held shields out solidly, interlocking together, while the Reprobi behind held their shields up, forming a protective "shell" over top of the Reprobi. They held this tight formation as they moved forward.

An eerie whistle sounded from within the formation. The formation broke immediately and the Reprobi charged, swords and axes drawn. Another whistle sounded and they formed into the wedge, sometimes referred to as a flying wedge. The offensive wedge in the shape of a pointy triangle was designed to smash through enemy lines and cause chaos. The key to the wedge was the speed in a tight formation. Like the tip of a pilla, it needed to puncture through the enemy ranks.

A hulking Reprobi that Rexus recognized as Mikmash, one of Lucivia's scouts, approached. His serpent-like flesh was pitch black and his eyes bright red. He appeared to have little difficulty walking. He carried a man dressed like a farmer, and who was missing a noticeable amount of teeth, hogtied behind his back across his shoulder blades. He dropped the man to the ground with a thud beside Rexus.

"We have one," Mikmash said bluntly.

Rexus grunted his approval. He got to one knee beside the man. "So, this is a ssson of Adam. Not very impressive." The man's head swung, swollen eyes going from Rexus to Mikmash and back, slowly widening until the whites showed all the way around. Rexus grabbed the near toothless man by the chin and forced the man to look at him. "I see by your clothing that you are not a soldier. This means I do not have to kill you. Tell me, human, what I want to hear and maybe you will live."

Rexus produced a dagger from inside his cloak. He pricked the man's upper arm causing a droplet of blood to roll down the man's forearm. The man's gut lurched, and he vomited a charming mixture of bile and his last meal. He looked as if his pounding heart would explode from his chest.

"What year is it since Jesus ascended to heaven?" Rexus said.

A short pause. Maybe fifteen seconds. With a quick motion, Rexus used his razor-sharp claw to saw off one of the man's ears. The man howled in agony.

"A little faster with your answers," said Rexus.

"1777!" Screamed the man.

The corner of Rexus' face twisted in a wry smile. "Now tell me everything!"

And the man did spill out everything, from his birth to this present day. Rexus stared at the man eye-to-eye as if deciding whether or not the men might have souls too, just like the Reprobi.

"To kill you quickly would be to reward you for the useful information," Rexus sneered. "However, we grow bored here. We lack fresh meat and entertainment. Tie him."

Long ropes made from braided roots were placed on each of the man's limbs. At the end of each rope was a Reprobi.

"Pull!" Rexus ordered.

Mikmash prostrated himself in front of Rexus. "Commander," Mikmash said. "My report: a large camp stands out with men dressed in bright red coats. They are clearly military." He hissed. "They appear to be different from the military men reported at the area the humans call Valley Forge. Their uniforms and accents are quite different. Perhaps they oppose each other? I do not know why they do not fight each other."

"Like us," Rexus said. "They probably wait for better weather to move. Blood runs quicker in the warmth. Tell me about their weapons?"

"Both armies have a few swords but most carry long metal pipes with wooden ends. I'm not sure what they do, but I believe these are their primary weaponsss."

"Pity, I should have asked the son of Adam before I dispatched him. Bring Atticus to me."

Rexus had Mikmash repeat his report then released Mikmash.

"What luck to come across two armies of mankind." Atticus grinned, his reptilian mouth a vile black, teeth twisted. "I see they have not learned after all this time to love their neighbor. They'll be easier to lay waste to while their houses are divided. I know you wish to attack when the weather warms, however, what is your plan?"

"We will wait until both these armies attack each other and then pounce after they have already been weakened. Get two bats with one stone."

As twilight approached, the sky darkened, and the Reprobi retreated to their shelters. Rexus listened to the wind howl as it fought to get into his shelter. *I will make the sons of Adam howl more than this.* The steady sound lulled him to sleep.

CHAPTER 4

FROZEN HELL

The early morning sun broke through the cracks of the forest, lighting up the dirt path ahead of the slow-moving column of soldiers. The motley assortment of men in mismatched uniforms snaked through the dark spruce forest on a barely visible snow-covered path. The trees, ravaged by the wind, seemed to lean toward each other, in the pale light, gloomily. A vast silence reigned over the land except for the suffering men plodding ahead. With each painful step, they were closer to Valley Forge, where they believed a treasure trove of supplies awaited them. Every frozen face was grim against the frigid wind, and on every mind were thoughts of warm winter quarters.

Captain Nathaniel Chapman took one step at a time, trying to ignore the pain, focusing on his steps. The hardness had already set in, of both body and elements. Every step forward was not without some degree of mental coercion. He wished they were steps closer to his home and family. He had been away from them a long time. As one of the first to take up his musket for the cause of liberty, he fought as a minuteman at the Battle of Concord and served under Israel Putnam at Bunker Hill. He watched a flag that fluttered next to him. The flag contained a green pine tree image in the center with the words "An Appeal to heaven" stitched above. Both the Revolutionaries and British pleaded for God's favor and intervention in this war.

By dusk, the army had settled into a clearing, flanked by boulders and trees. They tried to relax by the fire while they waited for food, but relaxation in a time of war is an elusive luxury. Exhausted men dozed to the crackle of the campfires. Their beds were where they stood before sitting down. For those awake, shallow holes were dug out, hot coals tossed in, then covered again with dirt, on which the men hoped to warm their bodies. It was never enough. The bone-chilling cold was always a grim reminder of the horrors of war, and for Nathaniel, his yearning to return to his family. The shadow of the tall trees and the glow of the fire reflected the mood of the men, that is to say with the exception of Ethan.

Lieutenant Ethan Davis was a new replacement sent by his Regiment. He was a thin man with dirt-blonde hair and deep blue eyes. He was undersized, about a foot shorter than average. Ethan displayed an unearthly positive attitude so much that Nathaniel figured Ethan hid something or was compensating for some wrong-doing in his past. Nathaniel pondered and pondered upon this, but failed miserably to find an answer. There was no way to puzzle out such an unyielding man of joy. In the end, he gave in; he figured it was simply his nature.

Nathaniel and Ethan shared a fire together. A private from their company stopped by to hand off a dented metal pot filled with their meal. He mumbled, "Another day of fire cake, and methinks I shall go raving mad. I crave juicy meat and fresh bread to sink my teeth into."

Ethan smirked as he took the pot. "Don't worry, your belly shall be filled up soon."

The man harrumphed as he walked away.

With a big spoon, Ethan scooped up a mash of flour then gently smeared a scoop on a stone at the outskirts of the flickering flames.

He turned to Nathaniel. "Are you in agreement there'll be plenty of food there?"

Nathaniel's breath was visible in the frigid air. "I reckon there will be, Lieutenant. Word is there shall be plenty of stores."

"It best be so." Ethan said. "I see about one in five soldiers hath no footwear and food is desperately short." Ethan grabbed the hot fire cake from the stone and passed it from hand to hand till it was cool, and then he ate, slowly nourishing with every bite.

Nathaniel picked up the pot, smeared his food then passed it to the men at the next campfire. As he watched the cake bubble on the stone, he caught the sight of brown flecks in it. *Maggots or weevils. It doesn't matter; they both taste the same.*

General George Washington and his youthful aide Lieutenant Colonel Alexander Hamilton approached the campfire. They held their hands out to the warmth of the fire. Even with the snowfall, there was no escaping the sight of Washington's signature Roman-shaped nose, the crease in his chin, and high forehead.

"Captain, I'm sorry to hear about the loss of your wife Elizabeth during childbirth with the loss of your newborn," said Washington. "It is a burden you should'st have to bear."

Nathaniel pointed to an available log. "Gramercy for your condolences, General. Would you gentlemen join us?"

Washington swept a handful of small rocks on the ground with his hand then sat. "You are young enough to start an issue again. It is not probable that I should have children by a woman of an age suitable to my own, should I be disposed to enter into a second marriage. Martha and I have tried, but I believe we are both unable. Regardless, I am fortunate to know the blessings of fatherhood. I have raised Martha's children as if they were my own."

Nathaniel was silent, unable to speak. Memories flashed through his mind. Washington patted Nathaniel on the shoulder and cast his eyes into the fire. He grabbed a stick and tossed it into the flames. The flames flickered and created red sparks that danced in the breeze.

"Hast you heard!" Hamilton said, sitting down. "We've been dubbed 'buckshot' by the British because we've been shooting so much of it and inflicting so many casualties at close range."

Nathaniel gave Hamilton a smile. By the light of the fire, Nathaniel could barely make out Hamilton's fair-skinned face with reddish-brown hair, deep-set blue eyes—almost violet. He had a strong jaw and a firm mouth. Little was known of the background of the 21-year-old Hamilton, but rumors spread that Hamilton worked his way up as a bastard child from the West Indies.

Ethan chuckled. "I don't reckon 'tis an ill name. I guess shows 'em how determined we are to hurt those lobster backs."

"Shall continue hurting 'em alright," Hamilton said. "Just wait 'till spring when we begin campaigning again. We shall win this fight. The Almighty shall deliver the colonies free from British subjugation."

Nathaniel caught the smell of burnt cake. *Oh, Fiddlestick!* He flicked the cake off the rock. It sizzled for a moment on the ground. He blew off the flecks of dirt and started to eat the charred food.

"General," Ethan said. The men can't wait to get to Valley Forge, warm lodging, and some good food."

Nathaniel spit out a tiny pebble. "This march hath been miserable on the men's feet. Hence many in blood-soaked rags. It would be great for them to be able to wear a good pair of shoes again."

Washington's face lost its color. He swallowed hard. Nathaniel could see Hamilton mentally working a way to help change the subject.

"Despite our best efforts," Washington said. "Valley Forge was raided by the British recently. Supplies unfortunately are pathetic at best."

Nathaniel winced as if he'd been stung. "If I may be so bold, why did we choose Valley Forge then?"

Washington's color returned to his face. "I picked the seat to watch Philadelphia, which is only twenty miles northwest of hither. 'Tis also far enough away to prevent a surprise attack by the British. We have yet another threat. It is not food or supplies nor the British now that we must fear, but the Grim Reaper that shall send his diseases." Washington was temporarily rattled by a cough. He caught his breath. "We will vaccinate everyone against the pox. I experienced smallpox myself when I was only 19 years old, on an adventure in the West Indies. I remember the chill running throughout the body, then within a few days a rash that erupted and covered my entire body. I'm pretty in my portraits but to this day I carry the scars on my face that reveal this experience."

Washington stood up, followed by Hamilton. "Gentlemen, I bid you goodnight. I appreciate thy office here. Take heart knowing the challenges ahead are worth the fight for liberty. When this is over and we are no longer bothered by the British, we shall build a lasting peace here that is woven in such a way that its foundation will never crumble." Washington and Hamilton walked away.

Ethan turned to Nathaniel. "Should'st we tell the men? Prepare them for the disappointment they'll find at Valley Forge?"

"No, if Washington wanted it known he would have told them earlier. Allow us not to take their hope away. It helps warm their hearts for now."

"Besides, you never know what tomorrow may bring."

"I know what tomorrow will bring. A whole lot of yesterday."

A sudden gust of wind howled through the camp, and freezing rain began to spit. More wood was tossed on the crackling flames, sending sparks into the night air.

Nathaniel came as close to the fire as he could, nearly burning his uniform. Several fifers started to play "Yankee Doodle". With eyes open and mind numb, Nathaniel dozed off to the melody. It was a restless sleep.

The next morning, after a quick camp clean-up, the army was on the march again. Relentless snow fell, making it difficult to see, and the wind screeched as it piled up snowdrifts. The men struggled, bent over against the cold, protecting their eyes with their arms. The surrounding forest looked blurry, then vanished, consumed in white.

CHAPTER 5

VALLEY OF DEATH

Misery loves company, and that company was encamped at Valley Forge, although it could have been renamed *Valley of Death*. There would be no celebration nor a holiday feast on arrival. The needed supplies were not there. The army of 12,000 poor souls with the addition of 400 camp followers made up of women and children were entering into a nightmare, an ice-cold one. It would not take long before death claimed its victims.

Most officers told soldiers to dig in the mud and kept their own hands clean; this was not Nathaniel. He was a leader that believed an officer needed to share in the hardships of his men. He believed it helped foster comradery and loyalty. You had to literally roll up your sleeves and get dirty with them. He currently was doing exactly this. His company was helping to build the earthworks that protected the encampment. Miles of fortification was needed as soon as possible, lest General Howe, Commander of the British army, be tempted to stir his force from their warm beds in Philadelphia. The first ditch that needed to be constructed was for the inner line defenses.

Nathaniel stuck a pickaxe into the cold and rocky soil. His face shown red from the bitter wind stinging it. He was by this time shivering and damp, not to mention hungry. He winced and grabbed his back before striking again.

"All right, lads, get your backs into it," bellowed Sergeant Abner Mulligan in a thick Irish accent. He lifted his shovel from the dirt and paused to glance over the men. He ran his hands through his unkempt brown hair that stuck in clumps, the paths of his fingers still visible right down to the scalp. A once robust middle-aged man, he had lost more than a few pounds recently and now held a sullen face.

Nathaniel looked up at Abner. "Sergeant!" Nathaniel snapped. "The men are weak from exhaustion and hunger. I fear if you continue to test the waters you may find yourself drowning in them. Keep the pace moderate, the trench will still be hither tomorrow."

Abner stuck his shovel back into the dirt. "Yes, Captain."

A groan followed by a thud was heard.

"You see?" Nathaniel exclaimed.

"Fetch a litter!" Hollered Abner. "And call fahr a wagahn."

The detail stopped working as they surrounded the fallen soldier. A well-worn wooden litter was brought. The makeshift litter had long carrying poles that hung with ropes, a wooden hammock. Archibald Montgomery, a private, was gently placed onto the litter. Archibald had definitely seen better days. His youthful, narrow face appeared pale and ghost-like. He breathed in shallow gasps.

A wagon approached that would bring the fallen man directly to one of many hospitals just outside the camp. A weathered farmer drove the small beat-up wagon pulled by a chestnut-colored mare. The animal was no stallion; it looked moth-eaten and old. The wagon kicked out clumps of frozen mud as it rumbled to a halt.

The small crowd cleared a path to let the litter through to the wagon. The gaze Archibald turned upon his litter carriers was so disparaging that Nathaniel nearly gasped. Archibald knew as did many the odds of returning from a hospital. Archibald was gently lifted into the wagon then covered in a pile of blankets.

Immediately, the wagon departed with Nathaniel remaining in the back of the wagon to steady Archibald on the ride. The driver tried to move as gently as possible, but the road made the wagon jostle back and forth towards the hospital.

Archibald moaned softly. "Sir, please tell my parents I love 'em."

Nathaniel's heart ached as he listened to these words. He looked into Archibald's eyes and shook his head. "Oh, fiddlesticks, boy! You'll be fine."

Archibald passed out.

On arrival at the hospital. Nathaniel helped carry the litter into the hospital, where a foul scent welcomed him, a smell of a butcher shop. Carts were crowded in rooms with little room to maneuver. They were directed to an available cart.

Archibald woke as they placed him on a cart. As they set him on the cart, he hurled his stomach contents over the side. He looked as weak as a newborn lamb.

Nathaniel patted his back, then sat at the edge of the cart. "I shall send a letter to your parents that you are ill and that you send your love to 'em. Now get some rest. Let your body heal; we need you in the fight."

Archibald barely registered Nathaniel's voice. His body shuttered then he closed his eyes.

Nathaniel held his ear to Archibald's mouth and listened. *Still breathing.*

Nathaniel waited until the doctor visited Archibald. The doctor silently examined Archibald. He didn't say what he thought, but his eyes gave him away. It wasn't good.

Nathaniel departed, knowing he would write the young private's letter that night and subsequently another one when he passed away. He refused a wagon ride back, preferring to walk instead. It was never easy to lose men in battle or to sickness. The walk he thought would help his mood, which was beginning to darken like the sky above him, but it did very little. His mood was a dark sea threatening to drown him.

Approaching the encampment, he noticed his men were already relieved of their duty. Only guards were posted. He walked into the camp. A short distance inside he abruptly stopped in his tracks, wrinkling his nose at the stench. His foot had lodged in a shallow latrine barely covered near a hut, located there because the men did not want to walk far in the cold. He did not gag. He glowered. *Discipline*, he thought. *The men need discipline.*

Tattoo or "tap-too" sounded on snare drums to signal the end of the workday. After removing his boots then banging the mud and filth off, he ducked his head as he walked into his crooked wooden cabin. The hastily-built cabin was one of the first constructed before the army began to freeze to death. At least he was one of the lucky ones whose cabin had a door. A fire—the only light in the cabin—was burning brightly in the stone fireplace. He placed his boot near the fireplace to dry.

Nathaniel sat on his bunk built into the side of the cabin; it was covered with a thin layer of straw, his mattress. Ethan lay on his bunk wide awake above him. Nathaniel glanced across the room at two empty bunks, where fellow officers had once rested their heads. But the illness had spread like wildfire in the cursed cramped quarters of camp. One lieutenant, Henry Alden, had died from high fever two weeks ago, practically overnight. His replacement didn't last long: Lieutenant Issac Winslow grew sick then suffered in delusional fever at the hospital until the Grim Reaper came for him.

It was only Nathaniel and Ethan that shared the cabin now. No replacements were coming.

Ethan looked down. "By the look of your brow when you walked in here it didn't hie well for Archibald?"

"No, it did not." Nathaniel crossed his arms. "Lieutenant, what was the final sick call count today?"

"Six, sir," replied Ethan.

Nathaniel shook his head. "If this keeps up, there won't be much of an army remaining to fight."

"At least some new tidings from this drudgery," Ethan said. "I received a visit from Hamilton when you were away at the hospital. Under advice from Baron von Steuben Washington hath made efforts to eliminate the filth of human waste and rotting carcasses of horses. Any soldier that violates his new rules on sanitation will be flogged. Also, all officers have been ordered to attend Steuben's model platoon review tomorrow. After the demonstration, this platoon shall disperse and train the entire army. The Baron is looking to create mirrors of himself . . . mini versions, so to speak. Although I doth find it funny, Steuben's flamboyant uniforms and cussing nature, I am unsure if he is the right man for the job."

"I hear tell," Nathaniel said. "Baron Steuben hath done a remarkable job training the men. The man flamboyantly served in the Prussian army as an aide-de-camp to Frederick the Great. He was one of 13 young officers chosen to partake in a special instructional course given by Frederick. Furthermore, he was a great tactician who was the architect behind many a victory in the Seven Years' War. If you bid me as long as he does his job he can cuss as much as he wants and dress any way he deems fit. I welcome any opportunity that would arise to turn the tide of the war in the Colonies' favor."

Ethan frowned. "I dist not know that."

Nathaniel looked up at Ethan. "Then perhaps you should'st learn to not judge so harshly before you have all the facts. Let's see these drills tomorrow and judge from what's presented."

Ethan said nothing. Nathaniel knew Ethan realized his mistake of judgment. He was a good officer. Ethan's once optimistic and positive spirit was slowly being removed the longer they stayed at camp. Nathaniel was feeling similar effects on his spirit.

Nathaniel fetched his quill, paper, and ink jar and penned a letter to Archibald's family. A little more of his spirit faded with each written word.

Outside the cabins, it was pitch dark with only the howl of the wind to be heard . . . providing one was awake, that is. The men encamped at Valley Forge slept soundly, unaware of what crept in the darkness. Dreams of men turned into nightmares as Lucivia lurked in the shadows. He moved quickly and with purpose, quietly collecting intelligence. He zigzagged around camp, counting the number of shelters to calculate troop count.

With the number counted he made his way out of camp towards the tree line. A congested cough echoed nearby. Lucivia crouched in the darkness to see the cause of the sound. He watched as one of Adam's spawns relieved himself of bodily fluid. An immediate temptation sparked in Lucivia's brain to kill the man, but he had been ordered by Rexus not to kill unless absolutely necessary. The pull was strong. He had wanted to kill a man for so long he could taste it in his mouth. *I can remain unseen and kill the human before he even knows I'm here. Their mortality should be tested. They were built in God's image, does that make them tough to kill? This information is necessary.*

Feeling justified in his thoughts, he followed the soldier, studying him closely. He wore a thick white shirt, ornamented with fringes. Tied around the waist was a broad belt, which was fastened to a pistol and a carved powder horn.

"Who's there?" the man called out in a gruff voice.

Did he hear me? Lucivia ducked behind a tree.

Lucivia thought quickly. "It's me, Peter," Lucivia said. "Would you give me a hand over here?"

"What do you mean to give you a hand at this hour of night?" the man said. "Hey, I can't even see you."

"Over here," Lucivia said. "I commandeered a barrel of rum. I just need a hand to lug it."

The man's voice lit up. "Alright, that's worth helping. By the way, your voice sounds like a. . . ."

As the man turned to look behind the tree, a glimpse of light that reflected off the moon showed the Reprobi's snake-like human form.

In a flash, Lucivia reached with one arm and grabbed the man, pulling him behind the tree. In his other arm, he pulled out his razor-sharp blade then stabbed the man in the gut. As the blood poured out, he hugged the man's body, using his hands to muffle the screaming. "

"Thanksss for the hand," Lucivia whispered in the man's ear.

Lucivia next plunged his gladius deep into the man's heart, and the man slumped to the ground. Lucivia bent over and kissed the corpse on the top of his head. *You may look in his image but there's not much of God within you. This is going to be easy!*

CHAPTER 6

STEUBEN

Outside, the mass of officers huddled together, for the wind wicked away body heat. To make room for the demonstration, the assembly stood in a large clearing outside the encampment. All officers including Washington and his attendants were present. Baron Friedrich Wilhelm Ludolf Gerhard Augustin von Steuben arrived at Valley Forge on February 23, 1778, and went right to work; they were excited to see the results.

Nathaniel and Ethan rubbed their hands together waiting to see the Baron. The heavyset man did arrive dressed as sharply and flamboyantly as ever, wearing a large medal of his own design, a giant eight-pointed silver star, etched with the word 'fidelitous'. His uniform was perfectly cut with a little ornamental frill on his cuffs and he wore excessive ornate holsters for his pistols at his hips. He held his tiny Italian greyhound Azor in his arms, wrapped in a blanket shivering from the cold.

Steuben handed off Azor to an attendant then addressed the crowd. "Le général Washington, vous remercie encore de . . . . . ."

Hamilton translated for Steuben. "General Washington, thank you again for the opportunity to serve the cause of liberty. When I arrived, the men seemed to lack everything, but not in spirit. No European army could have held together in such circumstances. The American soldier's independent nature is fierce and different from his European ancestors. You say to your soldier, 'Do this', and he does it. But I am obliged to say to the Americans, 'This is why you ought to do this,' and then he does it. With the military standards to meet their American spirit, the American soldier will be unmatched. I receive the model company made up of one individual from each unit is ready to disperse now. Allow me to demonstrate. Attention!"

As one, the men snapped into position. Steuben stopped at each man and briefly inspected his uniform. He turned to the crowd of officers and said, in broken English, "When the musket balls are flying toward thee, it is too late to adjourn and fetch anything."

After the uniform inspection, he put the unit through movements without firearms.

"Firm and precise movements!" hollered Steuben.

The men held shoulders square to the front and kept their backs straight, hands hanging down the sides, with the palms close to the thighs.

"To the Right—Face! To the Left—Face! Attention! Rest!"

With such precision, the men looked like they could march in their sleep. Next, they demonstrated firearms drills. The Baron shouted instructions, "Shoulder—Firelock! Present—Arms! Charge—Bayonet!"

Each motion was delivered with one perfect beat between each motion. Next, the men pulled out wooden drill flints and blank cartridges to simulate firing.

"Poise—Firelock! Two motions, Cock—Firelock! Two motions, Take Aim! One motion, Fire! One motion!"

To the amazement of the onlookers, they witnessed the model company's ability to fire off 3–4 shots per minute in a tight formation. Last, there came bayonet drills.

After the unit was dismissed, Steuben, followed by his translator Hamilton, conversed with the officers in attendance.

Ethan shook Hamilton's hand. "Simply amazing," he stuttered. "The men looked great."

Nathaniel patted Ethan's shoulder with an I-told-you-so look in his eyes.

Hamilton shook his head. "Don't look at me; I only translated." He nodded towards Steuben who was barely seen in the crowd. "It was the efforts of Baron Steuben and long hours spent that transformed the men. Besides seeing the trained men perform, 'twere also an example of leadership. Positive leaders, like the Baron, instill in their people hope for success and a belief in themselves. This army, once a rabble, a flock of scared sheep, is becoming a professional army ready to go toe-to-toe with the British. I don't know if I would go so far as to bid 'em lions, methinks. Ay, a pack of wolves, that creates a better vision."

"Allow us to hope," Ethan said, "we don't get all dressed up for naught. This can be the surprise we need to turn the tide. I was there during the Christmas Day victory against the Redcoats at Trenton. What a surprise we granted 'em then! This could hast 'em flat on their arses!"

"I am quite inclined to agree with you," Nathaniel said. "With this sort of training, perhaps the darkest days of this war will be behind us, and then we can truly seize the trophy of Liberty."

Hamilton's eyes twinkled. "We will find out soon enough. The surest way to find out whether our training will overcome the redcoats is to demonstrate on the battlefield. With the weather warming, we will soon see action with the army. I'm yearning to be on the front lines fighting for liberty."

Nathaniel was sure Hamilton had not seen much action. Nathaniel once thought battle exciting, but he knew now the exciting part was what you remembered when you looked back after the battle was fought. Not sure how to reply, Nathaniel politely nodded.

Hamilton moved on to talk to more of the attendees. Nathaniel and Ethan made their way back to their company.

The following day Nathaniel and Ethan watched Corporal Micajah Thorton, the company's participant in the model platoon, run his first drill with the sergeants of the platoon. He was a lean fellow with light brown hair and bony fingers. The sergeants were eager to participate after hearing feedback from Nathaniel and Ethan about the perfection they witnessed.

Maybe his musket was slick, maybe there was too much force in it; but on the Charge—Bayonet position, the weapon slipped out of Sergeant Abner's hand.

"Oh hell!" Micajah exclaimed with his eyes popped open. Abner turned to look directly at the exuberant corporal, and the sergeant's face flushed red with embarrassment. His face now pale, he retrieved the rifle that lay on the ground.

"Keep a tight grip when you stab," Micajeh said. "Let's see it again."

Abner held a death grip on the rifle while he repeated the maneuver.

"Good," Micajeh said with a smile. "Let's see it again."

Abner repeated the position. "I'm good. I bloody well gaht it."

Micajah faced him and with his best impression of von Steuben's accent said, "You must pe aple to do it vizout zinking. Arh! Verein zee bullets fly you must rely on instinct. Zis is why you ought to do zis. Arh! Und instinct I vill pound into you."

Abner harrumphed, shot Micajah an indignant look but repeated the position.

"Zat is good, Micajah said.

Ethan turned to Nathaniel. "Though our men will receive what I consider to be quality training, I do wonder what the British are doing in the meantime. I can only pray that the independent spirit of our soldiers the Baron spoke of will be a bolster to what they have learned."

"I have faith it shall," Nathaniel said. "If anything, we have that in spades. And faith can be a powerful weapon. Yet I believe the British have no idea what's coming for 'em. They are used to fighting amateurs; they won't know what hit 'em."

The drill instruction continued until it was perfect.

As the harsh winter gave way to warmer weather, the American fighting man's skills and spirits were sure to be renewed, but it was like Hamilton said: How successful they were would be proven on the battlefield.

CHAPTER 7

SON OF ADAM

The scent of fresh flowers lingered in a pocket of a deep forest. An angel stood with its heavenly glory, a picture of absolute perfection. No flaw nor blemishes marked this blessed being. Its skin was a brilliant white, like the ivory keys of a piano. A shimmering gold crown rested on its head. He was adorned in a simple white robe over a white undergarment. Beautiful white feathery wings curled up tightly on his back. With a trick of the light, the angel hid from sight to follow a son of Adam.

The son of Adam's face was sharply etched with his smile lines wove from his eyes and mouth. His long dark hair was held by a headdress, a feathered cap that had two feathers straight up and one down. He wore a cotton shirt, dyed a muted red, a short breechcloth, or loincloth, with a beautifully decorated apron panel attached in front and behind, leather leggings, and well-worn leather shoes.

The man stepped lightly as he followed a barely noticeable deer track. The noble buck paused, proudly standing with its majestic horns. He cocked the hammer on his musket, aimed, and fired. After a puff of black smoke spread through the air, he rushed towards the deer. It struggled to move, kicking its legs slowly. Taking his knife, he silenced the stag, releasing its spirit now and forever. Sitting with his legs under him, the man looked up, said a quick prayer of thanks, and then placed the deer over his shoulder. Following the deer path home, he felt an odd sensation of something tingling up his spine that he could not shake. A feeling of pure joy that made it impossible not to smile.

"Greetings, son of Adam," the angel said. Its voice was soft and gentle as if speaking to a beloved child.

The man froze. He was not overcome with fear, but an immense feeling of peace and tranquility, like serenity on the shore of a quiet lake.

"My time on this material plane of existence is brief," the angel said. "I will be short, to the point. Hear me, son of Adam, the prince of darkness goes by many names: Devil, Satan, Lucifer, Abaddon, and Evil One. Whatever you call him, know that this great evil one and his hordes have been released from their prison. They will come forth like a wave to destroy mankind. They are from another time in creation. They are immortal and cannot be killed. Even if you cut them to pieces, they would regenerate. But there is hope. They do have a weakness. This knowledge you must remember and pass on. If a trace of horsetail touches their blood, they will be returned to where they were banished to." The angel looked up. "Remember . . ." the angel's form began to diminish. It became translucent then completely vanished.

The man dropped the stag to the ground. With his eyes closed the man took a deep breath then replayed the words of the angel in his head. *God be praised. I have received these words from his messenger. This seed of knowledge, how to destroy the evil that is coming, must be passed to my brothers.* He opened his eyes, narrowed in resolve.

He ran through the woods, his feet hitting the soft forest floor. His lungs heaved and his body ached with the exertion but he was not stopping. Every fiber within him felt like he would burst if he didn't stop. Whether by chance or just dumb luck, he leaped off a large stone and fell hard. He heard a popping noise and felt a rupture of excruciating pain in his Achilles tendon. He lay on the ground, his face winced in a grimace. With effort born of sheer will and tenacity, he lifted himself up and continued in a limp.

As the light of day faded it became dark. The darkness was not a friend in this journey. The light was but was absent now. He pushed through the dark forest with no moonlight to help navigate. His heart beat rapidly, not out of fear of walking in the darkness, but out of fear of failure. He would give the information bestowed on him or die in the attempt. He kicked out with his good foot, feeling around for obstacles. One missed hole, a large stone or branch could end him. He used his hands as well. He groped around and shielded himself from the tree limbs that could take his eyes out. Eventually, he heard the sound of running river water he had been waiting to hear.

He quickened his pace only to catch a root sticking up from the ground which caused him to faceplant on the ground. With blood dripping from his nose, face stained with blood and dirt, he lifted himself back up. His legs kept asking him to rest, to find a cozy place to curl up and sleep but his brain willed them to move.

Taking deep breaths, he paused in front of the river that would guide him back towards his home in Kanonwalohale. His feet sank in the mud. The clouds moved, allowing some moonlight to escape and shine on the water. His eyes caught the ebb and flow of tiny whirlpools that were close to shore. He watched the current move briskly, bringing along any debris that could not easily escape its pull, wishing he could float away with it.

Eyes dilated, he peered around in the dim moonlight searching for the quickest path. He spotted a tall grassy area that appeared to be dry. With a *schmuck* sound, his shoes came out of the mud. With shoes and socks soaked in muddy cold water, he pushed forward.

The wind began to pick up with a howl, making an eerie sound as it blew against branches. A large cloud moved and covered the moon. Looking up, he prayed for the moonlight to show itself again, but the moonlight ignored him. The darkness made his other senses more alert.

He could smell the foul odor cast off the river shoreline. He could hear the frogs croak as they called for mates.

Abruptly, the river shifted to the north and he could not follow it any longer. His mind weakened against fatigue setting in, which threatened to thwart his mission. It called relentlessly for him to stop and take a break. The voice was gentle with soothing words. The voice of the devil, his heart believed.

As dawn's early light began to slowly appear, he quickened his pace regardless of the tears of pain that ran down his face. Dawn's light grew into the morning light. The good visibility was a blessing.

Unbeknownst to him, more bad luck would touch his fate. It seems evil was attracted to good like a bug to light in the darkness. The Reprobi scout Mikmash ran through the thick brush returning from a recon. He was not much of a scout, nor the best observer; he nearly ran into a man on a run. They both froze and faced each other.

The man stood wide-eyed gaping at the Reprobi. He could barely breathe, overcome with a feeling of fear and panic. The pressure in his head felt like it was about to explode.

Mikmash spit as he spoke. "Going somewhere? I don't think ssso."

The man's muscles knotted up as realization of his impending doom filtered in.

Mikmash slowly drew his razor-sharp battle axe over his head, a vicious-looking weapon with a spike at the back shaped like a serpent's tail. Then with an arc to the swing, he cut open the man's midsection. Blood and intestines spewed everywhere as the body fell limp to the ground.

Mikmash stood over the body. "I wish it would be over sssoon for you, but I'm afraid it will be more painful for you." Mikmash laughed and hissed simultaneously with satisfaction. "When you die, the animals will eat from your bonesss and defecate your body." He waved to the man. "Have a nice day."

Mikmash made no effort to clean his blade, simply placing it back in its holster loop. He lingered for a while, watching the man wallow in agony, then moved out.

The man sucked in deep breaths. Pain throbbed in his gut as he fought to stay alive. After several futile attempts to stand, he lay there in agony. He called out in a guttural cry, but no one answered. He mentally prepared himself to die. He had recently experienced the most amazing raw feelings he would ever know of peace, joy, fear, and panic. He reflected on what feelings his next life would bring.

CHAPTER 8

CHANGE AT KANONWALOHALE

The early morning sunlight stretched over the Oneida nation. The gentle light touched the strong wooden palisade of Kanonwalohale embracing it. The look of Kanonwalohale was different now, being indistinguishable from any colonial settlement. The warrior founders of Kanonwalohale—including Wolf Clan, Bear Clan, and Turtle Clan—had begun to drift away from time-honored Iroquois tradition. European agrarianism and culture were now a heavy influence at Kanonwaloha. Both men and women were awake tending their small farms.

Thomas Shenandoah strained as he carried a large stone. The sun glinted off his bald head except for a scalp lock, a crest down the center of his head. His lean muscles—built from hard labor and a good diet—flexed under his cotton shirt. The strain made him hunch as he carried it to a partially built wall on the border of his family's plot of land. He placed the puzzle piece carefully into position.

Years since I would not see myself building such a wall. The winds of change are coming. I feel it in the air. Change is a powerful storm that can't be prevented, yet haply it moves slowly here at Kanonwalohale. He took a deep breath and glanced at the tree line. He listened to the sounds of the woods. There were sounds but not as many as he once heard. Was he imagining this? *Yet something on the wind here is off, something recently has oppressed nature's balance. I cannot place it. Perhaps I have gone too long from its embrace. I shall enjoy a good hunt tomorrow. Not so much for the prey but to walk through nature and feel its blessing. Perhaps I will solve why I feel this way.*

As perspiration slowly dripped down from his face, he watched Agwalongdongwas—"Breaking of the Twigs," also known as "Good Peter"—approach. Peter was a devout Christian pastor and Warrior with a gift of incorporating traditional Oneida ideas and values into his Christian teachings so the people could understand his message.

"Good morning, Thomas. I have not seen you in church lately. Your brother Daniel attends without fail every Sunday, and your father every chance he gets. It is good to come and pray."

Thomas scratched his head. "I believe, but when I pray, I think he ignores me."

"If you are a believer and if you shall ever feel death's embrace, you shall be at peace in your heavenly eternity." Peter's voice became stronger. "He hears you. However, we can't begin to fathom his thoughts. We are but sheep led by a good shepherd. He chooses what prayers to answer when we call upon his name. He answers often; we only have to listen."

Thomas glanced down. "I will try to pray more."

"Consider that you do," Peter said. "We are at a time when we need prayer more than ever. Our nation is the smallest e'en with the recent addition of allied Tuscaroras. We oppose mighty foes, the majority of our former brothers in the Confederacy and the British."

Thomas stroked his chin. "I wonder if it was wise to leave the Confederacy. A wave of great peace has stood since Deganawida and Hiawatha founded the Confederacy after years of blood feuds. A peaceful society has existed for over 500 years. It was the Europeans' arrival that undermined us for the sake of greed."

"At the beginning," Peter said, "the Confederacy did not have to take sides in the colonial rebellion. But we couldn't work on both sides for long; they are our Christian brothers. Besides, it is done. As you know, your father and council of mothers have reached terms with Marquis de Lafayette, representing the colonists. They have just decided to send 49 warriors and one Polly Cooper."

Thomas blinked. "Polly Cooper?"

"Polly is coming to help with the corn donation to our starving brothers at Valley Forge, a donation of 600 bushels of white corn. The clan mothers insisted." Color flared on his cheeks for a flash then was gone. "Although this is a military trip."

Thomas wiped the sweat from his brow. "Polly is a force of nature. If she lacks something it is best to stay out of her way."

"I believe she shall make a great clan mother one day," Peter said. "If she learns not to be so headstrong. Mixing with Polly is like wading the streams. However peaceful the water looks; the bottom currents beneath can snatch you off your feet. I worry she takes too much of the burden of the nation upon herself. Like you, she often forgets that she is only one."

"Only 49 scouts?"

Peter nodded. "Yes, 49 scouts and one Polly Cooper. They asked for 2,000 warriors. We'll send what we can; we need our strength here to protect ourselves 'till Lafayette can help fortify us. Lafayette has promised that French Engineers will aid us. Your brother is among the 49."

"Of course he is. He always wants to be in the thick of it. "

"And you yourself do not?"

"Do not mishear my words. My father knows my desire. While I would be honored to be among those assisting the colonists, it is as you say: We will need as much protection here as we can possibly get. There is a possibility we could go against cannon. We must be prepared. We need workers to carry out the various tasks of labor required to fortify."

Peter nodded. "You make a most excellent point. Perhaps when Lafayette's engineers come to our aid, this will ease your burden."

"Regardless of when they come or not, I will go where I am needed, and at this moment, especially with my brother gone, I am needed here."

Peter said nothing more, and neither did Thomas. In the silence, Thomas was reminded of his feeling that nature was off. Peter turned to leave.

"Peter," Thomas spoke in a soft voice.

Peter turned around. "Is something troubling you?" asked Peter. "The look on your brow says you have more than the defense of Kanonwalohale on your mind."

Thomas bit his lip. "I feel a disturbance of some kind, though I cannot tell the exact reason. I feel the balance of nature is off as if a wound has been opened on mother earth. There is peace here, but I feel it shall not last long. The winds of change come like a mighty storm.

"Have you observed anything out of the ordinary?"

"Perhaps the animals. I see and hear them less. Our hunts are much farther than they used to be. I swear I hear fewer bird calls, e'en the crickets chirp less."

"Are we not approaching winter? Perhaps it comes early?" Peter questioned. "It should be quieter now."

"Yes, yet my gut says it's more than that."

Peter scratched his chin thoughtfully. "I will pay closer attention and I will pray on this. It is in prayer we find peace and understanding. And I suggest you pray as well."

Peter departed.

That night, before removing his blankets and laying on his bed's husk mattress, Thomas knelt in prayer. *Lord God, I know you are everywhere. I trust in thy presence, thy power, thy goodness, and thy control over all I'm facing. Help me walk through the questions, assured of thy answers, e'en though they're still unclear to me.*

Thomas dreamed. The dream was solid and realistic as a heart gives life. Although he was only a silent observer in the dream, he believed he was there. A bright white snake wriggled slowly through a barren field filled with short and tall dead, yellow grass. The serpent flickered its tongue, sensing its surroundings. It froze. A red snake, the color of fresh blood, of equal size, viciously attacked. It sank its fangs into the white snake's tail then proceeded to swallow it whole.

After the white snake was gone the red snake doubled in size. The red serpent began to worm away. Slowly it began to move with its tongue fluttering back and forth. It sensed danger and began to move quickly, rippling through the grass into a thick patch. It waited as still as death.

A black snake, dark as the blackest ink, of matching size, had observed the red snake's every movement. It crept up to the red snake then sprung into the air. Its fangs sunk into the head of its prey. The red snake went limp then was completely consumed by the black serpent. After doubling in size, the black snake slithered away.

The next morning the sky was cloudless and painted a vibrant blue. There was a gentle breeze, carrying the aroma of the forest. Thomas was breathing heavily as he followed a well-worn deer path. He heard a strange rustling sound and quickly notched an arrow, eyes unblinking. His senses were heightened as he moved, not making a sound.

He heard a guttural cry that sounded like a wounded animal. *No, it's a man.* Thomas ran towards the sound. He found a man, or what remained of him, torn and shredded with a pool of blood beneath him. He gurgled and coughed up thick red blood that trickled out of his mouth.

Thomas' voice trembled. "Jacob, is that you? Dear God, what has happened?" He knelt by Jacob's side in disbelief. "What h-happened?"

They locked eyes.

The look on Jacob's eyes could have penetrated the darkest souls. With sheer will, he clutched Thomas's arm. "Mm-mmust." Jacob spit up blood. He squeezed harder. His nails cut into Thomas. "Deee-mon, Hhh-orse-tail. Killl-evil."

Jacob's grip ended. His chest rose no more.

Thomas listened for signs of life, but there came none. He stood over his friend looking over the bloody mess. He was puzzled over what killed him and Jacob's final words. *Something sliced the hell out of him. I see a wicked slash. It doesn't look like a bear. An axe? A sword? What did he mean by Horsetail? His words must have been delirious, yet his eyes portrayed clarity.*

Thomas broke a large branch off a nearby oak tree and then snapped it in half. He removed his knife and cut up Jacob's shirt. With the strips, he secured the body between the poles.

Strength and heat filled his voice. "My friend, I know I should leave your body and deliver this message, yet I ain't leaving you behind. Besides your killer being present, you died alone. Have solace you shall go to our ancestors properly. Your graveyard will not be here."

Resolute, Thomas departed for Kanonwalohale.

Although he did not understand it yet, he found signs of the disturbance in nature he was searching for. The Reprobi were indeed a disturbance. A powerful creation that was not created nor intended for the earth. The wind of change on mother earth was about to move quickly and it sounded like a groan.

CHAPTER 9

LEST WE FORGET

There is strength in the mind that helps people accomplish great acts of determination. A resolved mind can be a powerful ally or foe. Thomas's mind pushed him beyond the normal limit of human endurance. With every step, the strain lit fire to his muscles, but Thomas pushed forward. He ignored his twitching muscles, focusing on just one step at a time. Images of Jacob's last words flashed in his mind. *What the heck was he talking about? Demons? But those eyes . . . those eyes . . . they had the look of certainty and clarity. Should I believe it even if I haven't seen it? What will my tribe think? Father and the elders will know what to do.* He swiveled his head back to look at Jacob. *We will be home soon, my brother.*

A distant dog barked, and another answered. Thomas arrived at the outskirts of Kanonwalohale. He traveled along dirt roads past farm pastures that covered most of the land outside the village's palisade. Translated from the Oneida language, Kanonwalohale means "Enemy's Head on a Pole" in honor of an enemy kill once displayed at its gate.

Before the wooden palisade gates swung open, Thomas was recognized. A handful from the watch ran out. They looked at Thomas and the litter he carried; expressions dark.

Thomas let go of the litter. "Please, I don't have the strength to run, send for my father; I need to see him immediately!"

A young warrior that had just reached manhood bounded off quickly to deliver the message. Warriors took over the burden of carrying Jacob's body. The gate swung open.

Thomas stood still taking deep breaths. He wiped the sweat from his forehead with his shirt sleeve. He felt wobbly and weak. But he was home. He would deliver the info to his father then rest. The fresh cool water was handed to Thomas in a deerskin bag. He gulped a majority of the water then poured the remainder over his head. As he shook his head, the water rolled off his bald scalp.

Friends approached to get an explanation of what happened to Jacob but he waved them off. A small crowd began to form as they waited for Thomas's father to arrive.

His father appeared, Chief John Shenandoah, along with his brother Daniel. They jogged towards Thomas. Shenandoah wore a traditional headdress, more a feathered cap that had two feathers straight up and one down to differentiate the Oneida from other tribes of the confederacy, and a beautiful braided leather necklace that displayed large bear claws, which adorned his neck. More distinguishing than his regalia was his face. The lines on his face etched the story of a hard life for the great leader. His eyes were those of a man who had lost what he knew he must lose, but that the knowledge did not soften them.

Thomas spilled out the grisly tale with every detail he remembered.

"I briefly saw the body of Jacob." Shenandoah sighed. "'Twere no common animals that did this. A remarkable weapon was used. The cut was deep and clean like a knife cutting through butter."

"And the words 'demon, evil and horse tail'—what do you think?" said Thomas. "We have to assume there is some kind of evil demon out there and a horse's tail is the defense against it?"

Daniel rolled his eyes. "Horse tails? Are you kidding me?"

Thomas gave Daniel a stern look. "I don't know why the horse essence is needed but I tell you it's important."

"God loves all his creatures," Shenandoah said. "Maybe the horse's essence is chosen because of its ability to serve? To serve is to love and love counters evil?"

Daniel folded his arms. "Surely, he was delirious when you came upon him. Demons are a fairy tale told to frighten us."

"You should have seen his eyes when Jacob told me this. I believe . . . no, I know . . . he spoke the truth!" exclaimed Thomas.

Daniel shook his head. "Then what are we supposed to do about it? We are stuck here waiting for the British or the Confederacy to attack us." He turned to his father. "We should be on offense."

"On this, I agree with you," Thomas said. "I'm tired of no action. The fight is out there."

Chief Shenandoah gave his sons a hard look meant to silence them. "I determined with counsel that it was best to defend ourselves and not join out in numbers, yet things hast changed. I see what happened to Jacob as a sign." He looked up towards the sky then took a long breath. "Allow us to take a path our enemies shall not expect. Thomas, gather all available warriors inside the palisade. Daniel, gather all the youth, elderly, those unable to fight behind these walls. Once this is done our warriors shall meet up with Washington's forces to grant him the tidings of what evil may be out there, then we shall hunt whatever killed Jacob."

Daniel puffed out his chest. "Time to sharpen our tomahawks."

Shenandoah frowned. "Not for you, Daniel. You shall keep watch over the tribe with the warriors that are unable to march."

Daniel threw his hands in the air dismissively. "I want to fight!"

"I know you do," Shenandoah said. "The warrior spirit is strong in you, but sometimes a warrior is needed for other reasons besides war. Now go! Off with the both of you!"

The bells of the palisade rang out alarm and word spread by wild-fire. Thomas and Daniel immediately went to work. Thomas with the assistance of volunteers began to gather all the available warriors of Kanonwalohale inside the wooden walls. Daniel began to gather those unable to defend themselves behind the protection of the walls.

When the majority of the warriors were present, Shenandoah addressed the warriors with a loud voice that echoed against the silence of the crowd waiting in anticipation for his words. "Based upon the seventh generation to come, it is in our best interest to gather our forces as one and leave the safety of Kanonwalohale. As war chief in full command. I give these simple instructions: Every warrior prepares to depart tomorrow at midday. Also, gather as many horse tails as possible, we shall tie 'em tightly to our arrowheads so they pierce and destroy this evil that has descended on us."

The sunset was low in the sky when Thomas staggered to his small, European, and framed clapboard home. He was miserable at this time, filthy and exhausted, not to mention hungry. After lighting his stone fireplace, he placed a tin kettle filled with water near the flames. He used the hot water and clean rags to wash the dirt and grime off his body. He then dressed in his nightshirt and made a small meal. With the flames flickered down, he pulled out warm embers with a poker then placed his copper pan on top. Mixing ground dried corn, water, and salt, he made cornmeal cakes on the pan.

On a well-worn wooden chair, he ate by the fire. After his last bite of food and after the crumbs were brushed off, he stared into the flames and tried to think. But his thoughts were as tired as his body and his body felt like it was trampled by a carriage. Sleep came quickly. That night, the white, red, and black snakes returned to his dreams, all consuming each other. The mystery of the images haunted his mind with no intention of stopping. He woke unable to shake them.

An hour before departure, Thomas made his way to the Oneida Stone, his favorite place to reflect and find inner peace. Perhaps in the serenity of the boulder's presence, he would find the answers to his nightmare. The granite upright stone was in the center of Kanonwalo-hale. This sacred "standing stone"—the Oneida were called "People of the Standing Stone"—was also a walking stone, for legend held that it followed the Oneidas whenever they relocated their principal village.

Han Yerry—Tewahongalahkon, "He Who Takes Up the Snowshoe"—a member of the Wolf Clan and a good friend, was already there. He was an Adonis of a man, tall and muscular. His head was shaved, leaving only a long crest of dark, brown hair with splayed feathers down the center. A respected warrior, he radiated danger the way a furnace gives off heat.

Han was a sachem at Oriska but recently moved to Kanonwalohale. Oriska and parts of the Oneida nation were more pagan and did not have as much support for the Colonists. Because of his faith, Han decided it was more comfortable to live in Kanonwalohale.

"How is your wife and son, and your wrist?" Thomas said.

A musket ball went through Hans' wrist at the Battle of Oriskany, August 6, 1777. The Yerry family was tough as badgers. "Two Kettles Together"—Tyonajanegen, his wife—and his son Cornelius also fought bravely at the battle.

"The wrist is good, my friend, as is my family," Han said. "I see we both have the same idea. This resting place for the stone often gives me a feeling of peace." He touched the stone. "The tidings of Jacob and that we must leave the safety of Kanonwalohale so suddenly gives much to reflect on. I worry about my family's safety without me. We hast ne'r been separated. My wife and my son shall stay behind to protect the palisade should'st our nation be attacked. They chose to keep so that when the fighting is done those that fought have a home to go back to."

"Your wife is a hardy woman and a good warrior," Thomas said. "She shall be safe within the palisade. My brother Daniel, although impulsive at times, is capable of leadership while my father is away."

Han's face showed he was not convinced of either. "You know what troubles me. I set my heart upon knowing what troubles you?"

"I have been feeling the balance of nature is off. Perhaps what killed Jacob is the cause of this. What troubles me the most is a dream I keep having that I cannot decipher."

"Tell me about this dream," Han asked.

"The dream is vivid. I dream about red, white, and black snakes devouring each other. I can't tell you why the dream bothers me so, nor can I even think about it without my stomach twisting. I feel somehow there is a message in this dream, a message I can't unlock. I thought that maybe it had something to do with our nation supporting the colonists. A warning not to split the confederacy over another nation's civil war and enter the conflict?"

Han paused for a moment, contemplating. He brushed his hand over his bald head. His eyes fixed on Thomas. "The great Peacemaker, Deganawidah, also had a dream or vision. He prophesied that a 'white serpent' would join a new people's lands and compose friends with 'em, only to mock 'em later. A 'red serpent' would later compose war against the 'white serpent' and after a time a 'black serpent' would later defeat both the 'white' and 'red serpents'."

Thomas pressed his hand against his temple and listened intently.

Han continued. "According to prophecy, when the people gathered under the elm tree, they were humbled, all three 'serpents' blinded by a light many times more brilliant than the sun," continued Han. "Deganawidah said that the 'red serpent' wouldst accept the 'white serpent' into their safekeeping as a long-lost brother. Perhaps the Colonists are the 'white serpent,' the British the 'red serpent,' and this evil we hunt is the 'black serpent.' I have faith in our efforts against the 'black serpent,' that it will not consume the land we trod upon. With horse tail, we have the gift of knowledge to destroy this evil."

Thomas mulled on Han's words. *If the black serpent is the final devourer, does this not mean this unknown evil will win?* His hands remained against his temple as he pondered Han's revelation. He chose not to tell Han his final interpretation of the dream that evil would win. Han was troubled enough worrying about his family's safety.

He looked up at the sky and glimpsed two small birds angrily protecting a nest from a large black crow. He watched the little birds dive and fight with abandon till the crow flew away. Watching the crow lose warmed his spirit. He almost smiled. Almost.

"I think you are right, my friend," said Thomas. "The Bible does tell us that he will set a table for us in the midst of our enemies, whoever they are. And though we walk in the shadow of the Valley of Death, we must fear no evil, for he is with us; his rod and his staff, they comfort us."

"Considering what happened to Jacob, going against Demons, we will surely need the Lord's help."

Both men departed to pack and say their goodbyes to those not coming on the march.

Every available warrior assembled at dawn with painted faces outside the wooden palisade. Chief Shenandoah separated those he deemed not fast enough to keep up with the march. Those would be added to those that chose to protect Kanonwaloha. The small army would be 350 strong. They wore mismatched clothing, mostly made of cotton shirts and short breechcloths or loincloths with a beautifully decorated apron panel attached in front and behind with soft, leather leggings and moccasins. They took every weapon they could find: muskets, bows, spears, and tomahawks. Without any great ceremony that would have been typical of such an expedition, they simply moved out. They ultimately did not know what they faced.

CHAPTER 10

FIRST BLOOD

The chill bit deeper as the sun started to fall below the horizon, which looked pinkish at this hour. In the dusk, a young Militiaman slouched towards his destination, glum, hands in his coat pocket. He relieved the sentry guard on duty just outside the trench that encircled most of the camp at Valley Forge and entered the small wooden shack with three sides and a blanket roof. A large wood stump served as his chair.

He sat down, placed his musket on his lap then began his watch. His body shivered as he fought to stay alert and awake. It was well known that if a guard fell asleep on watch, it was likely he would be shot. As a member of the Militia, he could leave as he chose, but if he was assigned a duty, he was expected to perform, and Washington did not take kindly to dereliction. He watched an open area in front of him that skirted along a dark tree line. Even with the light of a full moon, it was difficult to see anything, so he listened.

He heard a crunch of frozen snow. A shadow that formed into a dark serpentine creature approached quickly. The man became paralyzed with fear. His body shivered and a sudden choking sensation took hold of his throat as if hands were suffocating the life out of him.

Lucivia threw a punch, striking the side of his head.

The Militiaman fell off the stump to the ground unconscious, his musket falling off his lap. Blood dripped from his lip.

Lucivia turned the man's head and stared into his eyes. *What is so special about humans? They lack the strength even to resist the fear and panic we give off. What else? Well, best if I understand more. We can't infiltrate 'till we know their limitations.*

Lucivia's form began to fade into a gaseous cloud that seeped down the man's throat. The man's eyes rolled back as the Reprobi pushed aside his soul with its own. Lucivia slowly rose, having complete control over the man's functions.

Lucivia walked over to a large spruce tree and began to pound on it with his fists. He pounded until raw muscle and bones were exposed. Controlling the man, he had the benefit of not feeling any physical sensations of pain or pleasure. For a moment, he stared at his hands with blood dripping down his arms. He then began to run as fast as his legs would carry him in short circles. He stumbled awkwardly at first, but in short order, he became more confident. After that, he leapt into the air to test the strength of his leg muscles. *So pathetic. My Reprobi body, though ugly, is far superior to this pathetic shell.*

"What on earth are you doing?" a Continental soldier in a black tricorn hat said. He aimed and cocked the hammer on his musket's back. The soldier observed Lucivia's bloody hands, and his eyes bulged.

"I'm learning how to dance. Do you mind?" Lucivia sneered.

Lucivia grabbed the man with his mutilated hands then head-butted the man square on his face. The man's broken nose gushed blood onto the white snow. The man slumped for a heartbeat, but with adrenaline pumping through his veins, he managed to raise his musket.

Lucivia grabbed the end of the barrel covering it with his mangled hand. *This one has more of a fight in it.* A shot rang out. The sound echoed loudly in the silence. Lucivia did not even wince.

The soldier froze dumbfounded, with blood pouring from his face.

Lucivia stared at the strange weapon that fired. The scent of black powder lingered in the air.

"What do we have here?" Lucivia said. "Another one but much shorter."

Lucivia grabbed a pistol from the man's waist, pulled the hammer back, and fired point-blank at the man's chest. A shot rang out as the body crumpled to the ground.

Lucivia's eyes turned to slits. "Interesting weapon."

Lucivia bent over to examine the human body. It was barely breathing. The chest rose and fell slowly and its mouth gurgled blood. He placed a hand over its mouth till it breathed no more. *There is nothing special about them. They're as weak as the clay from which they were made.*

Remaining in human form, he went over to his Reprobi soulless shell. He strapped his gladius to his side. He then dragged his Reprobi form and the corpse into the debts of the forest. He let go of his burdens behind an old oak tree then searched until he spotted what he sought: a large black bear inside its den, a small cave in the ground, in winter hibernation. He prodded the bear with his gladius until the bear woke. Lucivia moved quickly out of the den. The beast growled viciously then charged out of its cave in fury. It found nothing.

The bear raised its head and sniffed the air picking up a strange scent. The scent was unfamiliar to it. The bear sauntered along, and then stopped abruptly. It stood on powerful hind legs, paws planted firmly on the ground and swayed back and forth. Lucivia appeared before it with a grin. The bear angrily exposed its sharp white teeth. Lucivia moved forward. The bear grabbed him by a large paw and with the other lunged for his throat. Lucivia pushed his hands forward in an attempt to hold the bear's mouth together. The attempt failed miserably, the bear bit his hand, tearing fingers off in the process.

Lucivia lay curled in a ball as the bear tore at his body, ripping flesh and clothing. His muscles wouldn't respond. The bear stopped beating and gave Lucivia a large sniff, and then began to walk away on all four paws.

Lucivia spit out a mouthful of blood.

The bear turned and quickly dashed back to Lucivia, with eyes set on finishing him. Lucivia unsheathed his gladius and stuck it into the bear's heart. The bear's body took its last breath on top of him. With great effort, enough muscles responded and he was able to crawl out. *Remarkably, I believe their minds can make a feeble body do more than their design. This is valuable information indeed. The human I have invaded still lives. I can sense his soul besides mine.*

He crawled back to his Reprobi form laying still on the snow. He slowly stood up. In vapor form, he poured out of the Militiaman's ravaged body into his Reprobi form.

The man in full possession of his soul again fell to one knee, coughing blood in an attempt to catch his breath.

Lucivia looked at the man curiously. He bent his arm, and with a twisting motion reached out and punctured the man's chest. His claws ripped out its heart. A light mist billowed from the heart as he held it. Blood and gore dripped off of it onto the ground. He flicked it into a patch of snow. *So fragile the body of a son of Adam. It is truly better for your kind to have masters to serve.* He tasted the human blood, as he used his long tongue to clean his claws.

Human voices were heard in the distance. He left the heartless corpse but hid the other body. He returned to the corpse to watch an armed group look over the mutilated body. He recognized prayers they sent to the Lord Almighty. He watched as the group discovered the bear.

Lucivia listened closely to a voice: "The Militia sentry must have heard something in the woods. He investigated to find a bear. He managed to slay the bear. Although for the life of me I can't find the blade. Probably fell to who knows where. Too bad the poor bastard didn't live to say his tale. It must hast been quite a story."

The group departed carrying off the body.

Lucivia took a large gulp of spirits then spent the night circling the human encampment at Valley Forge. Like a sponge, he absorbed all the information he could collect. Then he puzzled over the data. *Lucifer will be pleased with the knowledge I send back. Oh, human bodies are weak. They can be pushed over easily like blades of grass with a soft breeze. Yet I am not naive, I see the potential if their brains work similarly to ours. They will never be wolves; they are sheep. Sheep that need a shepherd to guide them. However, even a pack of wolves can be overwhelmed by a herd. Once started, a stampede is powerful. We must keep the sons of Adam divided.*

The sons of Adam carried off the body they suspected was torn up by the bear but they were unable to find the missing Continental sentry's body, only the red stains appeared on the white ground. Captain Nathaniel Chapman's company was tasked to search since the missing soldier was from their company.

The midday sun cast a scattered light within the trees as Nathaniel led his entire company to patrol for the missing soldier.

He pushed hard, against the numbness of the cold, feeling his undershirts clinging with dampness. With his musket in the ready position, it felt light at the beginning of the search but now felt like a pole of lead.

A flash of crows scurried away from the underbrush, startling the men. A soldier cocked his firearm and took aim.

"Delay that," whispered Nathaniel loudly.

The smell announced what Nathaniel wanted to see before him. On a single heap of chopped-up human remains sat a head. The frozen face was drawn and twisted, the face of a man who died in agony. Many men lost what remained of their breakfast.

Nathaniel turned to Abner. "Sergeant Smith, report to Washington immediately what we found hither. Apparently, the wildlife didn't do this. Probably the work of those Natives, those savage allies of the British. I didn't regard they would do such a thing under the influence of their British allies. Who would hast thought they could hast stooped so low."

"Whoever did dis, we will make 'em pay," Abner croaked. "A low-down shame it is."

Nathaniel gathered the patrol together.

He let out a long sigh. "This is not a way for a soldier to die. Let's bury the remains."

A shovel was fetched and a large hole was dug then the remains were transferred into the grave. A wooden cross was stuck into the ground and prayers were said. They filled the hole then piled what stones they could find on top. They wanted the grave to be located in case a family member or friend wanted to pay their respects in the future.

No wave of sadness took hold of the men as they returned to camp. Instead of sadness feelings of anger fed into them. Emotions boiled and festered in their hearts and minds as they pledged internally to make the British and their allies pay dearly.

CHAPTER 11

WASHINGTON'S FRUSTRATION

ashington's Headquarters just outside the Valley Forge encampment was a stone-walled modest house owned by Isaac Potts. The home was a two-story, three-bay Quaker-German village mill house with a foundation, a cellar, and an attic, as well as a one-story masonry kitchen extension. There was a roofed dog trot connection between the two. The house was rented to a relative of Issac named Deborah Hewes. Mrs. Hewes, in turn, graciously rented the entire house along with some furnishings for use by the Continental Army.

Despite the morning light coming through a window of the house, the room was still dark. Several candles fought back the shadows, giving just enough light to read. In a comfortable, well-made chair, Washington sat at his desk, feathered quill pen in hand, writing another letter to Congress. His army was still not getting what was promised. He was committed to the cause of liberty, but he felt the spirit of the Revolution from Congress was losing its backbone. He thrust his pen in the inkwell. He thought to himself with a short sigh: *Congress forgets we shall all be hung for treason if the revolution fails. Instead, some fester to replace me. The words written by Conway still sting my ears, arguing that I am a weak General, that maybe General Horatio Gates should replace me. Blast these politicians! If only I could, I would drag them by the ears, have 'em visit here and see the plight of the army for themselves.*

He finished the letter, and after sealing it with wax, pressed his seal, and then handed it to William Lee, known as "Billy," his trusted manservant and valet. He sat back down at his desk to continue writing letters. The candles burned low.

There was a gentle knock at the door.

"Yes?" Washington asked.

The door cracked open and Billy took a step in. "Colonel Hamilton to see you."

Washington placed his quill on the table and rose from his seat. Hamilton stepped in, raised his hand to a fist, and coughed lightly into it.

"General," Hamilton said. "The missing man has been found." He gave a detailed report about the gruesome discovery.

Washington's face grew disgusted, as he slammed his fist on the desk. "If this is the way gentlemen act . . ."

"I say, truly the British hast gone too far," Hamilton said. "They use savages to frighten us. This doth take the war to another level. This goes beyond a fight for independence and liberty. Both sides bid for God's favor, yet we are in the right. 'Tis good versus evil now."

Washington took a few long breaths and then sighed deeply. "The war hath not gone our way, yet I shall be damned now for sure would they win. I served the British power for many years. I can't receive they would stoop to such tactics. I know the Natives are smart and would not do this without British incentives. They're winning the war, so why would they do this?"

"Money. As sure as aught," Hamilton said. "Money and greed. They surely do not care about us; 'tis all about the profit to 'em. The quicker the war ends, the less it shall cost 'em. This is a war of economics to 'em. They don't crave to lose their cash cow. This land was taken, as

Caesar quoth: 'They came, they saw, they conquered.' And I would add: They took the spoils."

"Send out a dispatch to the papers immediately. This should'st convince loyalists to switch sides."

Hamilton immediately departed, and Billy stepped in.

"Dinner is served," he said.

Washington returned to his chair. He grabbed his quill. "I will take it at my desk."

There was no hiding Billy's disappointment on his face.

Washington's wife Martha entered within a blink of Washington's words.

"Billy said you will not be dining with me tonight?" she said.

Washington looked at his wife with fondness. She was five feet tall, slightly plump, with light brown eyes that appeared hazel to some. Her brown hair now was frosted with grey. In Washington's eyes, his wife would always remain stunning, but it was her wit and wisdom he fell in love with. Washington laid his pen down.

"I'm afraid I will be engaged all night toiling over my writing on military affairs and politics." Washington reached over and touched Martha's hands lightly with his. "Would I hast not made it clear, Martha, I appreciate all that you hast done to help me and I'm sure the soldiers appreciate your kindness to 'em, especially the socks you knit for 'em."

Martha blushed, and then bent over and kissed Washington on the forehead.

"My husband, I was hoping to have words with you at dinner. A friend of mine wanted to bring something to your attention. You know the camp followers hast no representation. They don't normally hast cause for complaint."

"What is it, Martha?" he said.

"Three women hast disappeared. Some left children behind. They truly vanished. 'Tis a big mystery over there without answers."

Washington frowned. "I believe I know who may be responsible. It sets mine heart to worry. I shall dispatch a brigade to guard the camp immediately. There shall be no more disappearances. 'Twere good you brought this to my attention. You are mine best eyes and ears."

Washington kissed Martha on the cheek.

She gazed lovingly into his eyes. "Mine dear, please do not keep up too late. You drive yourself too hard. You art no good to your men if you suffer a mental affliction."

"'Tis true," he said. "I stress about stress before there's even stress to stress about. I shall try and not be too long ere bed. Tomorrow, there shall be much to do."

Later, Billy found Washington slumped over his desk, sound asleep. Billy woke Washington with a gentle shake, and then led Washington to his bedroom. Martha was gently snoring. He helped Washington change into his nightshirt, and then placed a flat metal warming pan filled with hot coals between the sheets to keep the couple warm. Billy glanced at the couple briefly before exiting the bedroom. The spartan couple was a force to reckon with. He never met a couple like them, so devoted to each other and their love of others. He hummed a hymn as he walked to his bedroom.

> . . . . *Yet, saith the Lord, he loves us so,*
> *he brought forth George to marshal't us all.*
> *his hands shall wrack'd the British walls,*
> *they shout his name i' all the halls.*
> *an American Fabius hath been unleashed,*
> *to fight for liberty till it's complete.*
> . . . . *Yet, saith the Lord, he loves us so,*
> *he brought forth Martha to regard us all.*
> *her love and generosity are a beacon for us,*
> *to pester her thou had been nuts*
> *a daughter of revolution hath been unleashed*
> *to fight for liberty till its complete.*

CHAPTER 12

ASSASSINATION

Back at the Valley Forge encampment, tensions were elevated to a degree such as the men had never known before. It was bad enough that they had to retreat from the British and deal with ever-dwindling stores of supplies in addition to horrible diseases, but knowing that somebody or something—Native or not—had so brutally slaughtered one of their own was not good for their morale.

Nathaniel was more than a little pale just thinking about it, and Ethan, who sat down on a chair in Nathaniel's hut, easily took notice:

"Is something amiss, sir?"

Nathaniel sighed. "I feel as though this land we call 'America' was perhaps never meant to be. Between the routing the British have given us, and the fact that one of our own was so brutally slaughtered in a way that I could never have comprehended, I wonder if the signers of the Declaration of Independence understood what could befall us. Understood what the British were capable of doing to protect their empire."

"Nobody could have predicted this," Ethan said. We are irregular troops fighting a hardscrabble war against them. They are a well-regulated, officially sanctioned force. There is no way they would approve of what the Indians did."

Nathaniel blinked slowly. "Even so, I had hoped that us, endowed with the rights of Life, Liberty, and the pursuit of Happiness, could by opposing the British end the sea of troubles foisted upon us. I see now it may only be a dream."

"As lofty as it may seem to you," Ethan said. "I nevertheless have faith that we can somehow overcome the British and their Native allies."

Nathaniel raised an eyebrow. "That reminds me: about those dead men . . ."

Ethan tilted his head slightly. "What about them?"

"The men are in agreement that the Natives were responsible, yet deep in my heart, I have a feeling that someone or something far more terrible may be responsible."

"And what makes you come to such a conclusion?"

"I canst not say exactly, yet the way those men were grotesquely butchered, it seemed far too violent an undertaking for e'en the most savage Natives."

"Yet who then? Who didst that to 'em?"

Nathaniel shook his head. "You shall have the answer to that one when I do."

Ethan said nothing else. He simply got up from his chair and left, intrigued by Nathaniel's words.

Meanwhile, at a hidden Reprobi encampment, Lucivia reported directly to Rexus.

"I have passed your reports to Lucifer but I wanted to hear with my own auricles about your encounter with the Sonsss of Adam. Speak!" Rexus said as he gazed intently at Lucivia.

Lucivia prostrated himself before Rexus. At a nod from Rexus, he stood. "By possessing one, I have tested the humans' physical prowess myself," Lucivia said. "Their flesh is weak, and their bonesss are brittle enough that we may have them for our dinner." Lucivia's eyes grew larger. "But they do possess a strong spirit. If they can unite they may be trouble to us."

Rexus flickered his long tongue. "Bah! I appreciate your efforts but hold that thought to yourself. Lucifer will decide for us."

Lucivia crossed his arms. "The way the two armies war amongst themselves, they couldn't unite quickly enough that our golden opportunity will have been for naught. If we attack now, then this world will be ours for sure!"

"You do not know this for sure! Lucifer is against attacking now. What if humans know of some weapon or potion that can exploit our weaknesses? If we attack and that is the case, then we can bid adieu to all that we have fought to achieve! But I do agree, it is best that they do not unite. Perhaps there is something we can do."

Lucivia uncrossed his arms. "Then *what* would you suggest, my brother?"

Rexus stroked his chin. "These humansss . . . surely, there is at least one member among them whom they revere very much?"

Lucivia nodded. "As a matter of fact, in our reconnaissance, I discovered that amongst the humans who call themselves 'Americans' there is one in particular whose name is often spoken as if he were a god..."

"Do tell me," Rexus said.

"These 'Americans' call him 'George Washington'."

"Interesting. What else can you tell me about this 'George Washington'?"

"I'm afraid I do not know much," Lucivia said, "but they consider him a grand strategist, and they have much faith that he will be able to lead them to victory against the ones in red, whom they call the 'British'."

"Then it's decided. If you can somehow assassinate George Washington, make it look like the British did this, then perhaps the Americans will be demoralized to such a degree that they will easily capitulate to us, and never assist the British, and the rest of the world shall fall to us soon after."

"With your permission, I will make arrangements."

"I will get the permission of Lucifer. As his chief scout, he will listen to you. I'm not particular on the when or where, only that you do it in a reasonable amount of time."

"Right." Lucivia bowed his head then quickly headed off to make preparations.

In a modest house not very far from Valley Forge stood the headquarters for the army and General Washington's private residence. The sun had gone down for the day, and most of its inhabitants had gone to sleep save for a few men selected to perform watch. The selected were from Washington's Guard or the Life Guard, initially created by selecting a select few from each Continental Army regiment. The purpose of the unit was to protect the money and official papers of the Continental Army and more importantly to protect Washington.

Though the Americans had accounted for the British in choosing this house for army HQ, they hadn't enough foresight to account for more otherworldly forces, and it was thanks to this that Lucivia was able to effectively penetrate the exterior of the house by turning into his gaseous form and seeping through a small crack in one of the windows. Now that he'd gained entry to the house, all that remained was to find Washington and kill him, making it look like the British did it. He could have easily overpowered the occupants of the house, but that would've been very messy, and surely such a mess would've been discovered, which would, in turn, put the Americans closer to awareness of the Reprobi, which would mean they would be more apt to align with the British—as Rexus said—would bid adieu to all they had fought to achieve. On the other hand, owing to the fact that the house relied on candlelight for interior lighting, Lucivia found himself more easily able to sneak about the house.

Lucivia found himself approaching one of the sentries from behind. The sentry was dressed in a blue uniform with a leather helmet adorned with a medium blue cloth binding and a white plume tipped in blue placed on the left side of it. Lucivia caught the sentry in a yawn and possessed the sentry. Though he despised having to take on such a mortal form, he knew it was necessary to complete his mission cleanly and quietly. He walked about the house, trying not to draw too much attention to himself as he searched for Washington. A search of the first floor proved fruitless, so he went upstairs to the second floor, and it was here that he seemingly struck paydirt: A sentry stood guard at one door. Without hesitation, Lucivia approached the sentry.

"Seth, you know General Washington can't . . . Seth!? SETH!"

With one quick blow, Lucivia punched the sentry in the throat. In seconds, Lucivia snapped the sentry's neck and he went limp. Lucivia quietly but quickly dragged the sentry's body into an empty room, then went back to Washington's bedroom. He opened the door slowly and entered a dark room. He sensed what he thought was Washington, so he checked his possessed body for any suitable weaponry. Finding a pistol, he withdrew it, cocked the hammer, and . . .

"Hey, what are you doing in here!?" shouted a voice behind him.

Lucivia spun around, only to spot another sentry with a pistol. His gaseous form spit out of Seth's body just as the other sentry fired—a direct hit to the head thereby ending Seth's life and awakening Washington.

"Huh . . . ? Wha . . . ?"

Still bleary from sleep, Washington tried to get himself together and at the same time try to figure out why he was awakened.

"Caleb, why hast you disturbed me from my slumber!?" said Washington.

Major Caleb Gibbs, commander of the Life Guard, lowered his pistol. "Sir, Seth here was trying to kill you."

"Kill me!? I thought this nonsense was over?"

Caleb and Washington both knew this was not the first attempt on Washington's life. Within months of the Life Guards' formation, numerous enlisted and non-commissioned officers had been in the middle of what has become called the Hickey Mutiny. Several individuals of the Life Guards, together with Sergeant Thomas Hickey, had been arrested. Hickey, an Irish migrant who had abandoned the British Army, reenlisted the Continental Army. The court-martial testimony towards Hickey was enough to convict him. He was sentenced to death and hanged on June 28, 1776, and became the first member of the Continental Army executed after an official court-martial.

Caleb shook his head. "I thought it was, General. I thought it was." Gibbs tapped one of the buttons of his uniform, the standard designated regimental number on the uniform replaced with the word stamped "USA".

As if Washington did not have enough to worry about, Washington would have another urgent stressor added to his list: whether the British had enlisted certain Americans to turn their backs on the new nation and betray the Revolution by deposing him as commander of the army.

CHAPTER 13

HUNT FOR RECOMPENSE

A ny brotherly love towards the British was shattered after the failed attempt on Washington's life. Anger towards the British boiled like a hot kettle about to release its scream of steam. Anger was also mixed with fear. Fear of what lengths the British were capable of going to win the war. Slowly the anger and fear were joining to make hate. Hate is darkness; once descended, it is difficult to lift. Darkness cannot drive out darkness. Only light can lift it. Light is eternal, and always there, but it is often not sought until the darkest hour.

Early morning, under grey clouds, reveille sounded with a shrill call from bugles followed immediately with drums roaring for a call to arms. The men stumbled to get dressed and out the doors as quickly as possible with their muskets in tow. Sergeants hollered at the men and directed them to assemble in parade formation. A roll of thunder bellowed through the air. The clouds dropped a deluge just as the men formed, a hammering downpour.

George Washington sat on his horse facing the army with tiredness in his eyes. Eyes that said the weight of the world was on his shoulders. He ignored the rain although it dripped down his face and slicked his hair to the scalp. The men hunched against the cold, faces haggard but excited to hear what he had to say. Washington's breath was visible in the frigid air.

"The British have begun moving out of Philadelphia," Washington said. "We march now to take the fight to them and their Native allies. We owe them recompense!" He drew his saber. "The sons of liberty march ahead to victory! We will hit 'em hard! No reprieve! No quarter!"

In a brief flicker, whatever weariness displayed in his eyes vanished as he drew his saber and held it high.

The army erupted in shouts of "Huzzah!"

With a thud of his heel, Washington galloped along the line. The army hollered and cheered till their voices were hoarse.

The rain-soaked army was drawn in a long column of four rows and marched out to pursue the British. They kicked up mud as they marched, most of the soldiers were covered with it, and the air was thick with a pungent smell.

By the late morning, they arrived in a heavily wooded area. They crunched over branches and early growth of spring. A strong scent of a wet forest filled their noses.

Washington and his entourage of aides rode slowly along the side of the column. He stopped at short intervals, greeting the men and making short conversation. He stopped at Nathaniel.

"Captain, I am saddened by the tidings about the brutal slaughter of one of your men. Although I am no more enlightened as to the identity of the perpetrators, I assure you that you have nothing but my utmost sympathies, and I am absolutely committed to ensuring that this Revolution succeeds, along with punishment to those that committed this vile act."

"Thank you, General, for your sympathies," Nathaniel said. He rubbed his chin. "Sir, some of the men—and I—suspect that this might not be the work of the Natives. The damage done to the corpse seemed too brutal to be their handiwork. Are they not influenced by Christian ways?"

"A most curious development," Washington said. "Although I do wonder who could have committed such a heinous act if not them?"

"The remains were studied. There are still a few men who cling to the imagining that some sort of animal was responsible, yet they canst not put a finger on a specific animal."

There was no hiding Washington's look of doubt. "An animal slicing up its prey then placings the victim's head on the pile?"

Nathaniel lowered his shoulders. "I know it must sound crazy."

"We may never have our answers. Let us focus on the hour at hand. Stay the course. The British need to be dealt with. We will engage the British, Lafayette will take the lead advance. I will remain with the main force, as is your company. Be ready."

"Yes, sir."

The rain slowed to fat drips then ceased entirely. Wet uniforms were uncomfortable to march in but nothing compared to the suffering recently endured at Valley Forge. The winter spent there so cruel would quickly be forgotten; the future was all that mattered. Why blame the rain? The rain only knows how to flow downwards.

The men plodded on, resolve in their faces, every step closer to settle the score with the British. A re-shaped Continental Army in performance and spirit, especially with Baron Steuben's training, were confident they could match the British on the battlefield and pay them back for atrocities they committed.

Nathaniel kept a watchful eye over his company and the surrounding forest.

"Eeek-aahh," screamed Quill, like a little girl. Quill was a private in Nathaniel's company, an energetic, thin man known to tell tall stories.

Nathaniel turned towards the laughter. A slack-jawed Quill had stepped on a rotten branch and a red and black garter snake slithered its way out from underneath, startling him. The private's face was bright red as laughter abounded. Nathaniel couldn't help but smirk as he watched the scene unfold.

The entire Continental advance was halted.

Abner removed his tricorn hat and whacked the closest man. "Lads, forbear this ruckus or you shall hast extra misfortune on ye. Ye restrained all of the column, ye asses! There are eyes i' thy heads and none i' thy spuds."

The column reformed and continued. The drums and fife took up a tune.

The army sang as they marched.

> *Let Tyrants shak their iron rod,*
> *And slav'ry clank her galling chains,*
> *We fear them not,*
> *We trust in God,*
> *Our God Forever reigns.*
> *Howe and Burgoyne and Clinton too,*
> *With Prescot and Cornwallis join'd,*
> *Together plot our Overthrow,*
> *In one Infernal league combin'd.*
>
> *When God inspir'd us for the fight,*
> *Their ranks were broke, their lines were forc'd,*
> *Their ships were Shatter'd in our sight,*
> *Or swiftly driven from our Coast.*
>
> *The Foe comes on with haughty Stride;*
> *Our troops advance with martial noise,*
> *Their Vet'rans flee before our Youth,*
> *And Gen'rals yield to beardless Boys.**

---

* Song inspired by "Chester," a patriotic anthem composed by William Billings

Crows began to circle above in anticipation of blood lust. Prior to nightfall, the rebel force arrived at Barren Hill. Under the light of a full moon, the army set up camp on the high ground, near a church, facing south with the artillery in position for defense. In the morning, they would seek vengeance.

CHAPTER 14

ALTERNATIVE MONMOUTH

The rebel army caught up to the British near Monmouth Courthouse, New Jersey. To Lafayette's chagrin, Major General Charles Lee replaced him to lead the advance. Lafayette joined the main force with Washington. Lee was originally offered command but refused, not understanding the importance of his role in the attack. When he learned he would take charge of one-third of the army he begged for the opportunity. Washington decided to place his trust in the veteran. He hoped Lee would strike a heavy blow and the main army would simply clean up after the engagement.

The main force waited under dark grey clouds that moved in to cover the sky. A self-induced fog of fear grew thick as it attempted to dampen the men's fighting spirit. They strained their eyes at the movement of shadows. They listened to every sound. The sound of a bird chirping, which the men had become used to, began to occur less, then stopped entirely.

A rider dressed in a Continental uniform appeared in a full gallop toward the army. The ranks broke to let in the rider. He clutched his shoulder with blood seeping out, his face a look of panic and terror.

"Those lobster backs are on my tail, boys!" the man said. "Save yourself! The redcoats have taken the field, they smashed through the lines. It's butchery."

The rider maneuvered through the main force until Washington grabbed him by his scruff and shook the information out of him. His story was soon confirmed by a few soldiers slogging down the road, then hundreds came, some collapsing from exhaustion as they made their way to safety.

An astonished Washington could not figure out why they were retreating. He questioned every officer he could find but found no coherent answer. At last, down the road, Charles Lee came down the road covered in dust. Washington, face red with rage and hand white-knuckled clutching his saber, confronted Lee. "You, sir, are retreating in considerable disorder, with the British advancing behind you. What the &#%!, &#%!" Washington unleashed a volley of cuss words at Lee, to the astonishment of those listening, before ordering Lee to the rear.

Washington then kicked his horse, galloping forward, and began the difficult task of rallying Lee's disordered troops and forming them into his force before the British assault led by General Charles Cornwallis.

Under the roll of drums, the men formed lines. On the left side of Nathaniel's company stood Washington's Guard in blue uniforms, along the right side was a Rhode Island Militia regiment that proudly brandished a pure white banner, which carried a heavy anchor in the color blue with the word "Hope" embossed above. Washington was not with his Guard. He took a regiment of Lee's previously fleeing Continentals along with two full New Jersey regiments to advance up Englishtown Road up the slope of Perrine's Hill to position cannon and have a reserve force ready at a moment's notice.

British drums were heard, and the British were seen as they advanced in tight ranks moving to the march of the beat. The British advancing wore their bearskin caps, making them appear tall and menacing. These soldiers, their elite grenade and assault troops, advanced slowly in perfect step, then halted just opposite Nathaniel's position.

"Steady, men!" shouted Nathaniel. "Bear the line! Remember your training, and remember the atrocities they have delivered unto us! Make ready!"

"Take aim! Fire!" was shouted from the British direction.

Shots rang out. Men fell quickly as the grenadiers opened with deadly, accurate fire.

Nathaniel pointed with his saber. "Fire!"

The first rank in his company fired, then worked to reload quickly as musket balls whisked back and forth. With a red spray, a soldier winced, and then fell to the side of Nathaniel.

The woods filled with the smoke and the smell of discharged powder. Nathaniel exhaled hard to clear his lungs from the smoke of gunpowder. With a groan, another Continental soldier close to Nathaniel fell.

Suddenly, Nathaniel heard a spluttered cry from the Rhode Island Militia line, "Fix Bayonets!"

Nathaniel was perplexed. *What the hell are they thinking? Well, I guess 'tis what the redcoats would least expect.* "Give 'em hell!"

Nathaniel hollered, "Fix bayonets!" and his orders were quickly echoed over the clamor of fire. Washington's Guard echoed the same and the echo continued throughout the entire army.

"Charge!" hollered someone from the Militia.

The British scrambled to dress ranks as the Militia struck, followed by Nathaniel's company with the entire Continental Army close behind. The front ranks of the British crumbled then the armies broke apart and slugged it out. It was absolute chaos. Man to man, bayonet versus bayonet, with the horrible groans and screams of men being stuck like animals. It was war at its worst, both savage and bloody.

Nathaniel parried a musket that would have been a mortal blow from a grenadier, aimed at his heart with a bayonet strike. With his block, he became off balance then fell to the ground face-forward. He spun to his back, removed his pistol, and shot the attacker point-blank in the chest. The man staggered but did not fall. Scrambling to his feet, Nathaniel stabbed the attacker in the throat with the tip of his saber. Blood poured out from the grenadier as he futilely clutched his throat to hold back the blood. In the time it took to draw a quick breath, Nathaniel just barely dodged another bayonet from a British soldier with eyes of pure hate. The attacker managed to hit Nathaniel with the butt of his weapon, and Nathaniel slumped to the ground clutching his head, his saber dropped from his hands. The attacker reversed his weapon with his bayonet about to plunge into Nathaniel. Nathaniel uttered a quick prayer as he prepared to receive death's embrace.

There was a muffled thud. The attacker took a round in the chest and he stumbled, and his bearskin hat fell from his head as a few more shots tore into him, finishing him off. He collapsed in a heap.

A line had formed behind Nathaniel controlled by a screaming Lafayette.

"Dress in rank! Dress in rank!" Lafayette repeated until he lost his voice.

Nathaniel bent low to the forest floor. He could feel the blood dripping from his head. Blood mixed with dirt clouded his vision.

"Captain! Are you alright?" Ethan said as wiped the gunk from Nathaniel's eyes with his hat.

Nathaniel stumbled slightly as he regained his bearings. He watched the Continental line reform behind a heavily stained banner that spelled the words "Don't tread on me." He drew strength from the passing banner and grabbed a musket laying on the ground. He fought back pain and raised his weapon. His target was a British officer that stood in the front ranks pushing his men to mass in formation. He fired. A red splatter and the officer fell with a wound to his eye.

Under man-made clouds of black powder smoke, the two armies killed each other unmercifully.

With the Continental Army to the South and British to the North, the Reprobi army watched the battle unfold as they moved into position. Situated to the east, they watched the bloodshed with hunger burning in their veins to join in the fun. The Reprobi army was spotted, but at a distance, they looked like enemy reinforcements to each army, either militias or loyalists.

Rexus remained still as he watched the humans clash from behind a tall, thick oak tree. He did not see much through the fog of smoke created by musket fire. He was able to hear cracks of musket and rifle fire and witness bodies drop as a result. He looked down at the gladius strapped to his side. *Would we have been better if we brought our entire army? But what do we have to fear? Are we not immortal? Lucifer be praised in his wisdom; fewer numbers show our strength. The Sons of Adam will pile up like stacks of dead branches.*

He ran through the Reprobi offensive strategy one more time in his head. They were waiting for the best time to pounce on their unsuspecting prey. When the battle was the most engaged. The surprise would be their ally. They would quickly attack then encircle the two armies then the slaughter would begin in earnest. It would be dirty up close as combat. They would see life fade from their victim's eyes, eyes knowing God had abandoned them. By destroying two armies simultaneously, they would make the Sons of Adam know they could never match the Reprobi. Future armies would simply surrender. The rise of the Reprobi would begin and the earth would be theirs as it should always have been.

Rexus took a deep breath, muttered to himself. "It is time."

He came out of the shadow of the tree into the dim forest light and with a snarl on his reptilian, snake-like face cast a terrifying gaze. Bright red eyes reflecting off the light. He drew his gladius and shouted, "Death to the Sons of Adam!"

Out of the shadows of the forest, the Reprobi came out, formed ranks, then advanced.

In the thousands, a volley of pilas rained down at the center of the American and British battle. The sharp tips cut through bone and muscle like a blade through butter. A second volley was released to the same devastating effect. After the barrage, the Reprobi closed in tight ranks with shields overlapping. They marched forward in quick steps as they called out mockingly in lizardly tongue: "God has abandoned you! Witnessss the rise of the Reprobi! Your mastersss are coming!"

Both the British and Continentals stared dumbstruck at the advancing wave of Reprobi. To many, the sight was either a dream or simply their imagination. To some, it struck them with anxiety and panic.

When they drew in close enough, the Reprobi's tight ranks exploded into a charge, and they roared as one. In sheer terror, the men beheld death approaching in hideous forms. With gladius and battle-axes, the Reprobis tore into the human ranks. Men could scarcely believe what fell on them. Stunned at first, both armies bled, slaughtered like a pack of wolves among sheep. Men in the thick of the fighting ran from the carnage in terror but were blocked by the thousands of men on the battlefield.

As the initial shock wore off, the Continentals and British began to fire a few shots at the Reprobi. Musket balls and rifle shots tore through shields hitting the hideous creatures, but the Reprobi were undeterred in their butchery. The damage to their flesh seemed negligible, barely an eye blink caused by the hits.

The British and Continentals abandoned any grievances they held toward each other. They began to melt ranks together quickly against a common enemy. Regiments on both sides not engaged, standing at a distance, watched in confusion. Panic and fear filled them as they watched the bloodshed and carnage but they managed to hold their positions.

The Reprobi with eyes of madness unleashed fury pent up for thousands of years. They hacked and tore at the men with bloodthirst. Blood seeped into the earth to mix, forming a gory mud.

"What the . . . !?" Nathaniel tackled a man fleeing in terror. "We have a better chance if we stick together! Hold!" He dragged the man off and pushed him to a line forming.

The man ignored him, refusing to move. Nathaniel raised his pistol in the air and fired. This caught the man's attention. The man ran to the line. Gradually, men began to assemble.

He could hear Sergeant Abner hollering at the men. "Comb ahn, boys, get it tahgether ahr you'll meet your maker!"

Nathaniel caught Lafayette at a short distance, forming his men then moving towards him. Together they formed a ring, bayonets out.

In the midst of battle, gradually, the fear of the Reprobi began to subside. The angst of death was more terrifying than the Reprobi.

Lafayette left the circle, rallied a few hundred men including a British regiment then formed another circle with bayonets out. The British blended seamlessly. It was hard to imagine only moments ago British and Revolutionaries were killing each other; now the former enemies stood side-by-side, facing terror. Concentrated musket fire, hundreds of balls, began to pound the Reprobi, at which point their assault began to slow. The Reprobi had nearly encircled their foe but a gap remained.

A solitary Reprobi at the front of their ranks dropped his shield. He broke free carrying a vicious-looking battle axe. He charged toward Nathaniel's ring of men. He took multiple hits. One took out his eye with a splatter of goo but kept coming. He was now inches from Nathaniel. He raised his axe above his head. A murderous look in his remaining eye.

An arrow sliced through the air and struck the Reprobi, puncturing deep into his shoulder. Another arrow pierced his neck. The creature roared in frustration, pulling out the arrows as if they were annoying toothpicks. Another arrow struck into his remaining good eye, simultaneously another pierced his heart. His legs buckled, and he crashed to the ground with a loud thud.

Shots and arrows rang out from the woods, tearing at the Reprobi's front ranks, many taking multiple shots. Some found their way in the armor's vulnerable spots. With a loud battle cry of "Oonah, oonah," Oneida warriors appeared. They attacked fiercely and savagely. They quickly leaped into close combat with tomahawks and spears. Their ferocious, almost suicidal attack staggered the Reprobi and gave them pause, which the British and Continentals took advantage of with massing fire.

The British commander General Lord Charles Cornwallis was killed. The highest-ranking British officer Lieutenant Colonel Henry Monckton rattled his saber calling for "Retreat!"

"Retreat" was echoed through the ranks. Chaos ensued. Both armies began to panic and run. Nathaniel got in the way of a runner and took a punch to his head. He took the pain and slashed the attacker across his face with his saber, causing the man to take off screaming. A movement caught him from his side, and he turned to stab. A native covered in war paint stood in front of him, his face set like a bow.

"We reckoned you could use some help," Thomas shouted over the noise of battle.

Surprised, Nathaniel shot Thomas an indignant look.

Suddenly cannon fire thundered and cannonballs began to move through the air. One ripped the head off a Reprobi, leaving his lifeless form flopping on the ground. Blood and chunks of flesh splattered.

Thomas rubbed his bald scalp. "I do not think the horsetail is working!"

Nathaniel looked at Thomas quizzically. "What are you talking about?"

"Never mind!" Thomas said. He pulled off a tomahawk from his belt then rejoined the battle royal.

Nathaniel watched the battle unfold like a slow-motion picture. As he did blood from his brow dripped on the ground. For now, he fought the wooziness of his wound with adrenaline pumping in his veins. He caught sight of Lafayette working helplessly to form a line to cover the retreating men. He ran to his side.

"Now is our chance!" Nathaniel said. "The cannon will cover us!"

Lafayette nodded. "Agreed. Let's make haste."

Nathaniel and Lafayette worked together. They called out while swinging their sabers in the air amidst the confusion. Some soldiers took notice, while some ignored them entirely. Those that did would later perish.

The army of combined Continentals and British escaped through the gap, limbs moving as fast as they could. Neither looked back.

CHAPTER 15

RETREAT

The Continental Army footslogged back to Valley Forge accompanied by Native American rescuers and more than a few British in tow, in fact nearly their entire force. They traveled along a small road they thought would conceal them from the Reprobi. The dirt road was low to the ground with plenty of forests to hide it from plain sight. The walking wounded trudged slowly at the rear of the retreating column. A few were carried by litter, but mostly, they used makeshift crutches and volunteers bearing the weight of their comrades.

Multiple messengers by swift horse were dispatched to Valley Forge. They carried news of defeat by the snakelike creatures that called themselves the "Reprobi." There were messengers to give the news and those to reinforce that it really happened. The Reprobi sounded like nightmares. Nightmares out of children's stories come to life. The messengers arrived safely.

Despite their defeat, the Continental and British armies survived, those who remained lucky to have escaped with their lives. They owed a great debt to the brave charge of the Native warriors. There was a great history of many debts never collected by them. Only time would tell if this debt would be repaid. Once engaged the Oneida warriors fought furiously like mother bears protecting their cubs. Hearsay and rumor had spread the word that they had a secret weapon to deploy and had they known it would not work they never would have made the near-suicidal attack. However, what did it matter, the action was done and the day was saved.

Nathaniel scratched the dirty cloth bandage wrapped around his head. One of the drummers from Nathaniel's regiment, a tall boy for his young age of 13, stood close by his side, fearful that he would collapse from his head wound. He did not have much support, especially because the boy would not keep quiet.

The boy sputtered, "Didst thou see those snakey demon things? Their heads looked so snakelike. Yet those eyes. Those eyes were human. O, they granted me a fright. Didst thou hark what they bid us? 'Sons of Adam!' I reckon I am one. Don't we all join from Adam and Eve? Didst thou wot 'twere Washington who advanced the cannon to help us 'scape? Didst thou . . ."

Lafayette approached. "Enough boy. From the look of him, this officer has a pounding headache already."

Nathaniel smiled. "Thank you."

"Don't mention it," Lafayette said. "I'm sure your head is pounding enough. You didst well in the broil. I owe debt besides a thank you for your service."

"And I thank you," Nathaniel said. "No debt is owed. We helped each other. Although I wish we could hast saved more. A shame to have abandoned so many wounded on the battlefield." A tear began to well up. "If only . . . ?"

Lafayette patted Nathaniel on the shoulder, his expression softened. "You are not the only one to share that burden. It pains me also. Alas, the burden of the living must be our priority now."

Lafayette walked away. He approached a nearby wounded red coat, who was missing his right hand. It was sliced off by a Reprobi. "I praise you for your service." He continued to walk through the body of men, giving encouragement and praise.

Without Lafayette's protection, the drummer beside Nathaniel became chatty again.

Carts and wagons met the severely wounded partway to Valley Forge then took them directly to surrounding hospitals, the last place on earth soldiers wanted to be. Hospitals were feared as a place of death for wounded soldiers. For some, a loss of a limb was a death sentence. It was common practice if a limb was badly putrid or fractured to amputate it, and only a third of amputees actually survived the surgery. There were no painkillers and most of the patients were given alcohol and a stick to bite down on while the surgeon worked.

After the wounded were collected, the remaining men entered Valley Forge. Dozens of fire pits smoldered in the camp as men recovered from the fog of battle as best they could, mostly in colorful conversation about the battle against the unearthly creatures, perhaps sprinkled with a hard drink of rum or two.

On arrival at camp Nathaniel gladly dismissed the drummer boy and began to walk to his former cabin. His head throbbed but he had work to do. He was confident the wound would heal. The blood on the wrappings was dry. As he approached his cabin, he spotted a few from his company meandering outside.

Washington passed by on his horse and noticed Nathaniel's bandaged head. He stopped then turned around to face Nathaniel. The horse snorted.

Washington looked defeated, ground down to paste. A look of concern in his eyes. "Looks like a nasty gash on your head. There is plenty of blood soaked in your wrappings. Compose haste to have that looked at, cleaned, and some new wrappings."

Nathaniel stuttered, "I am good, General. I must attend to my men."

"I will see to that," Ethan said, looking up at Washington. He was beside Nathaniel.

Nathaniel turned to Ethan. His face was in awe. "Lieutenant, it is good to see you. I thought we lost you in the confusion of our escape."

"As you can see, I'm alive and I'll look after the men for you while you mend." He looked up at Washington." I'll see that he gets care, General.

Washington nodded then rode off.

Ethan called out, "Sergeant!"

Abner approached.

"Escort the captain," Ethan said. "Compose sure he gets his wound attended to."

Nathaniel looked at Ethan pathetically.

"Sergeant, you have your orders," Ethan barked.

Abner looked at Nathaniel. "Come ahn captain, de sooner yooehr wound is looked at de sooner you'll be back."

Abner found a wagon then commandeered the driver to fetch Nathaniel to the nearest hospital. Then he returned to help Ethan.

The driver took Nathaniel to Yellow Springs Hospital, a converted health spa where local physicians had once sent patients for therapy in the bubbling mineral waters. Under Washington's orders, it was currently undergoing improvements, including the construction of a three-story building. The inn and several barns served as the hospital for now.

After entering the largest barn, there was no escaping the pungent odor of blood, body odor, and dried straw in the air. Nathaniel navigated around patients in makeshift beds, examining the outsides of medicine chests looking for a wrappings label.

A woman noticed his pathetic search attempt. She gave him an eagle-eyed stare. There was something familiar about her appearance. She held her hair high in a knot, parted in the center, and waved back on both sides of her brow. She was plainly dressed in a red gown and bloodstained blue petticoat worn over a second hooped petticoat, which kept her skirt out. Her cheek had a small scar just below her eye.

Recognition. Nathaniel's eyes lit up. "I know you. You're Molly . . . Molly Pitcher?"

Her face seemed to crack a slight smile at the sound of the name. Then her face went stoic. She shook her head. "Another one that knows those stories. I'm in no mood for humor nor being called nicknames." Her tired-eyed face said she was in no mood for any conversation. There is a certain amount of tiredness that equates to madness, and she looked close. She drew a deep breath then softened her tone. "How may I help you, Captain?"

"I'm looking for clean wrappings for my head. I hast bled through these."

"Come with me," Molly said. She walked off not looking back to see if Nathaniel followed. "We are in desperate need of medicine, but we should have plenty of wrappings to spare."

He followed her through the cramped and crowded space. The sound of hacking and moans of poor souls could be heard everywhere. They stopped to make way for a soldier brought in, removed from his litter, then gently placed on an available wooden cart.

Molly pointed to a well-worn chair. "Take a seat." The look on her face showed there would be no compromise.

Nathaniel sat. "The wrappings?"

"The way your current wrappings look, you will be examined." Molly pointed to a linen sheet covered over a body. "This one thought his wound wasn't that serious."

She gently removed Nathaniel's bandage. "You are lucky the wound is not that deep."

A Native American woman squeezed by Molly and Nathaniel at that moment. Her beauty caught Nathaniel's attention. As she looked down, he caught her eyes. Her eyes were a deep, earthy brown, the color of rich soil after pouring rain. She was dressed in a long skirt that was decorated with beautiful beads and purple-dyed porcupine quills. He remembered that her two braids signified she was not married.

After moving past them, the woman stopped abruptly then made direct eye contact with Molly. She spoke in her thick native tongue with a few words barely discernible in English. Whatever she was saying she spoke with an air of confidence.

Molly gave her a warm smile. "I will." Then she looked at Nathaniel: "Polly has volunteered with many others to help us with the wounded. We are so grateful for their help. She doesn't trust the doctors very much. She has prepared a honey dressing for one of her people named Thomas, yet after looking at your injury, she feels you shall need it more. She desires you to have it. It should'st help prevent infection."

Nathaniel grinned as he fumbled for the right words. "I am honored. Prithee let her know I would be grateful if she applied her dressing."

Polly applied the honey dressing mixed with herbs, and with her tender hands, the application did not hurt. After the wound was re-wrapped with a fresh cloth, she crossed her arms then gave clear instructions to Molly on what she wanted Nathaniel to know about his wound care. Then she left without a second look at Nathaniel.

Molly translated the instructions to keep the wound clean and to change his dressing as often as he could then she rolled her eyes slightly keeping a faint smile. "On your way out near the entrance, you will find a table with plenty of cut shirts donated for use. Take what you need. Good day to you, Captain."

In a blink, she was gone attending to more patients.

Nathaniel caught a wagon ride and returned to his men just as darkness set in. He found them by the campfires. They were scattered in clumps of five or six men around a fire using wood stumps as seats. He noticed an occasional red coat or a Native American mixed in with them. He sat down and stretched his legs before a freshly lit campfire with three privates, who graciously welcomed their commander to join them. The men did not stay long; they departed for guard duty. The Valley Forge watch had been quadrupled since arrival.

Sitting on the ground he watched the dance of the orange and yellow flames leap hungrily for fuel. He added a small stick to the fire, watched it catch flame and hiss. As he absorbed himself in the crackling of the stick and the woody fragrance of smoke, his thoughts drifted off the day's events.

Ethan slumped on the log next to Nathaniel. "Sir, it's good to see you back from the hospital. I hast the count."

Nathaniel knew what count he was talking about. "Proceed," he said after a soft sigh.

"Three we know died for sure, we have witnesses. Fifteen men are missing. We presume they fell in battle. Ten wounded. Maybe a half shall make it back, the rest ain't probably going to compose it." Nathaniel shook his head as Ethan continued. "A few red coats hast joined our company on account they hath been separated from their units. To be honest these units were most likely wiped out during the battle. Abner is with 'em now, showing 'em the ropes. While you were away, we received decrees directly from Washington. At morn, we shall be on the move. He does not crave to be a sitting target."

"That makes sense," Nathaniel said. "I wonder what the hell we went against. I'm sure they're puzzling it out at the top. Seeing what we're up against doesn't fare well for us. They ran through us like we weren't e'en there. At the close range with 'em, we don't stand a chance. If the Native Americans didn't help us and the cannon fire at the right moment we would have been slaughtered like cattle. Killed to the last man methinks." Nathaniel paused, reliving through the horrible memory. He averted his eyes to change the mood. "Guess who I met? That Molly Pitcher."

Ethan's eyes opened wide. "Fancy that?" He coughed. "The one I told you about?"

"Indeed, it was her, the scar beneath her eye marked her," Nathaniel said. "Doth tell the story again."

"We call a few Molly Pitcher but Mary Hays makes 'em all look bad," Ethan said. "Known for carrying water to the thirsty soldiers even with bullets flying. She survived a grapeshot blast with only a small laceration below her eye. Her husband was part of the artillery, who was then attached to a cannon at the Battle of Monmouth. I witnessed her drop her water jugs to help attend to her husband at the cannon. While in the act of reaching a cartridge and having one of her feet as far ere the other as she could step, a cannon shot from the foe passed directly 'twixt her legs without doing any other damage than carrying away all the lower part of her petticoat. She didn't e'en flinch, just continued to help fire the cannon."

Nathaniel began to tell the story of his hospital visit.

"Polly, you say?" Ethan interrupted. "I think that was her who came earlier handing out corn and teaching us knuckleheads how to prepare it. Oh, I saved you some. You must be hungry?"

"To tell you the truth, I'm famished," Nathaniel said. "For food and answers."

Ethan shrugged his shoulders. "Food we have. Answers I'm afeard we have none."

Ethan handed Nathaniel a small leather pouch filled with cooked corn niblets. "I'd offer you a drink of rum yet Washington hath ordered no drinking tonight. He doesn't crave men to wash their troubles in a drink."

With dirty hands, Nathaniel popped them in his mouth one by one as he continued his story.

"Honey dressing?" Ethan said. "Is that so? I would heed her instructions. Natives know a lot about nature, herbs, and such. They hath been here plenty before us colonists arrived. I hast some extra linen I can cut up for you. Mine mom's a bit of a cracker. She sent me bedclothes. Do you receive that? Does she regard us on a pleasure trip hither with bed and comfort? Ha!"

The site of Abner brought a smile to Nathaniel. Abner sat on a small mossy stone near the fire. He turned to Nathaniel. "Captain, 'tis good to see you back with us." He pulled out a bottle of rum from his coat pocket. Ethan gave him a baleful eye and he quickly put the bottle away.

"'Tis good to be back." Nathaniel said. "Although a damn shame to learn we have lost so many men. How are the new recruits coming along?"

"The lobster backs will be fine," Abner said. "Till dey rejoin deir mates. I reckon some of our own soldiers are mixed with deir fahrces. Ne'r thought I would see the day of us wahrkin tahgether."

"Nor did I," Nathaniel said. "However, in light of our new foes, I feel it prudent that we should work together for the time being. We'll sort out our differences later."

Abner nodded. "After what we went against, you bet I'll be believin dat!"

As the sun went down large amounts of wood were added to the fires. As if they feared what could be hiding in the dark. The fires became bright and vivid, as though someone had shown a spotlight on them. As the night grew longer, they added more wood. There was tension in the air. Not silence. Voices spoke softly as they eyed the darkness warily.

A loud voice cackled laughter followed by another. Hoots and chuckles began as the men joked and traded stories. They relaxed, puffing their pipes. Tension was leaching out slowly but would not be erased.

Many chose not to close their eyes, fearing nightmares. Late into the night, they laid on their backs until darkness was cut only by the guiding light of the moon and the light of the flickering flames.

CHAPTER 16

REPROBI AFTERMATH

Thunder boomed through the sky and lighting rippled in long streaks as if unhappy with the unworldly presence of the Reprobi. The rain sprinkled down, unable to wash the filth from the earth. The Reprobi felt the cold hard droplets touch their skin. This strange sensation gave them little pause as they stood on the blood-soaked earth, finishing their work.

The air was full of scents of death. Blood pools. Dead flesh. Corpses lay where the men fell like discarded corn husks. The Reprobi chopped them with their axes. The heads were removed and piled up into piles by the thousands. The heads stood in grotesque faces, blood dripping off them, mixing in pools of muddy water. Crows and carrion began to hover under the dark clouds. Soon, they would feast on flesh and pluck out their eyes. The art display was left to strike fear in the hearts of humans. This type of mutilation on a grand scale had not been seen since Vlad the Impaler, hundreds of years ago.

Rexus stood looking at the pyramid of heads, clenching both his fists. Reprobi went about their work, avoiding him. His second in command, Atticus, had no choice.

Atticus prostrated himself. "The healing is going well. The most mutilated, 24 of them, are in holes filled with dirt. The first few have already climbed out. The ones missing their heads will be longer. Perhaps several weeks."

"We failed to crush the human armies," Rexus said. "With our failure, they will now combine their strength. Three distinct forces will join as one!"

Atticus looked down. He kept his voice hissingly soft. "We came ssso close. If we had more numbers, we could have finished surrounding them and prevented their escape. We would have churned them into pulp."

"Do not question the Prince of Darkness!" Rexus snapped. "He does everything for a reason. Do you not see, there is victory in knowledge. We tested their abilities against us. We will be ready next time."

"These weapons they carried are astonishing." Atticus grabbed a musket off the ground and snapped it in half over his knee. "We will have to learn how to manufacture these weapons, turn their technology against them."

Rexus gave a wicked fangful smile. "Those cannons were truly magnificent. I saw a single iron ball take a limb off a torso with ease, and the multiple balls—grapeshot, they call it—effectively delivered both pain and misery. With weapons like that, we could destroy and conquer much quicker."

"We will have them. I know the Lord will want to study then use these wonderful weapons." Atticus looked at the pyramid, a pleased smile on his face. "Our work here is done. What are your orders?"

"Have Lucivia's scouts keep an eye on the human armies, I want to know every move they make. Also, I want his scouts to collect a few Sons of Adam for questioning. It's time we talked to each other. Do we not both share the blessing of speech?" Rexus touched the handle of his sheathed dagger. "I will bleed every word out of them!"

"The more we know our enemy, the . . ."

Rexus continued, ignoring Atticus. There was blood lust in his eyes. "They will not be lucky next time we meet. We will kill every last one in the next battle, destroy any notion in them of ever opposing us. They will fear us and fearing us will be their first step to worshiping and serving us."

"Shall I send word to our Lord about the battle with the Sons of Adam?" Atticus questioned.

"No, I will return to hell myself and give this report in person." Rexus waived his clawed hand. "Now go!"

Rexus made his way back to hell alone. Although this hell was not a hot place, hate and bitterness towards the Sons of Adam kept it plenty warm. For the first time, a guard was posted outside Lucifer's chamber in case the impossible happened and a human wandered in. Rexus pressed his fist to his heart, returning the guard's salute, ignoring the fact a guard was posted at all.

Lucifer sat on his throne tapping his red reptilian fingers on the stone arms. His face looked peaceful and confident. As if the earth were already his. His eyes grew with excitement as Rexus entered. Rexus prostrated himself before the throne then with a wave from Lucifer he rose. By the look on Rexus' face, Lucifer knew immediately the outcome of the battle. The Reprobi were defeated, but he needed to understand why.

"How did the battle go against the Sons of Adam?" Lucifer asked.

Rexus fought the temptation to not make eye contact. He had wanted to return with good news for his Lord. "The battle did not go as expected," he said. "The human army escaped to fight another day. The Legion fought well, but we were constrained by our numbers. If we went up against twice their numbers, we would have been the ones who had to escape. Our brothers count on the entire Legion to be used at the next confrontation."

Lucifer harrumphed. "I thought they would ask. If I have learned anything from our prison sentence, I have learned caution," Lucifer said. "I only sent out half the army. We did not know what time had brought the Sons of Adam. Deploying half our strength gave us more flexibility and options. What if the battle had turned against us? I still do not understand God's plan. Although I feel he allowed us to escape and he wants us to rise." He clenched his right fist. "As long as we are free from our prison, we have all the time we need to take this world. And they will be ours as it should always have been."

"Our brothers do not doubt you; they are only disappointed that the Sons of Adam escaped. They expected a quick victory. We have put fear into the Sons of Adam but I feel we must judge them differently now."

Lucifer's eyes flared. "Do we fear them now? We are immortal!"

"It is not *them* our brothers fear. The Sons of Adam were not even dust when we were created. They are more technologically advanced than we anticipated." He lifted a musket off his back. "These weapons they carried in battle stung like annoying insects. Useless against us unless it hits a vital area, but against them, against their weak human flesh, it is extremely deadly." He handed the musket to Lucifer. "They have gigantic versions of this. Huge cylinders that can fire at a great distance. Cannon, they call them. We experienced them; they shook the very ground. If they mass and hit us point-blank, they can easily push us back in battle."

Lucifer inspected the musket. "Interesting. We will immediately study these weapons, work to replicate them, then use them when ready. But we will not delay our attack waiting for them. Our rise continues. Our strategy shall be to get close where they won't have any advantage, so close that we can grab them by their bootstraps. If we can gain the element of surprise, then all of the cannons in the world won't be of any help to them!"

Lucifer stood up straight then removed himself from his throne. "I will use the entire Legion. I will personally lead my brothers to glory."

Rexus prostrated himself low to the ground. Pure joy sent shivers throughout his body. He was at a loss for words. He could only smile.

The call to arms bellowed throughout hell. The remaining brothers would join the rest of their brethren.

CHAPTER 17

UNITE TO SURVIVE

Three flagstaffs marked Washington's command tent. One flagstaff held the Union flag with red and white horizontal stripes and thirteen stars in the left-hand corner. The other two banners were on shorter staffs. One was the white silk flag of Washington's guard that depicted a guard holding a horse's reins, a woman personified as Liberty leaning upon the Union shield, and an American eagle. The second was a yellow flag depicting a snake and the words "DON'T TREAD ON ME."

To say the tent was crowded was an understatement. A large dining table rested in the center of the room. It was a little unbalanced. In haste, the legs were forgotten and the table was held up by piles of large stones. Lieutenant colonel Alexander Hamilton, Major General Marquis de Lafayette, Major General Charles Lee, Brigadier General Benedict Arnold, and General—also Pastor—Peter Muhlenberg stood around the table with Washington. More than a dozen aide-de-camps stood behind them.

Washington slammed his fist down on the table. "No, we shall keep our command mobile and forswear Valley Forge. Would we are still and they surprise us, they will wipe us off the map, then there shall be naught to protect the people. We must focus on defense, yet at some point, we shall want to begin thinking of offense. To resist them, we must have answers. Where doth these creatures come from? What brought 'em hither? Why may they be riddled with shots and still keep moving forward?"

Pastor Muhlenberg cleared his throat. "General, I say to you the truth, 'tis this war against brothers that hath set this evil among us. They're not human, that much is clear. They are some type of ungodly creatures. We must pray fervently for God to save us from this evil. We must put on the full armor of God so that we can take a stand against the devil's schemes."

"And pray we shall and take action," Washington said. "One thing for sure, gentlemen, the revolution is over. It ends today, hither and now! This is now a war to save mankind. We are literally walking now through the valley of the shadow of death. We might not but be at the end of times. " Washington turned to Lee. "Immediately open channels with the British. After this meeting, dispatch three letters with three riders to them. My letter shall beseech 'em for an immediate truce, a present end to hostilities, and a summons to meet urgently. We must unite together to stand a chance. The enemy of my enemy is my friend."

"I agree," Muhlenberg said. "The British may not always be on our side, yet they are fellow Christian brothers and anti-evil. 'Teacher,' quoth John from the Bible, 'we saw a man driving out demons in thy name and we told him to stop because he was not one of us.' Jesus told 'em, 'Do not stop him, none who doth a miracle in mine name can in the next instant say aught ill about me, for whoever is not against us is for us.'"

Washington rolled out a map of the former colonies on the table. Hamilton held the top of the map so it did not roll back up.

"In the meantime," Washington said, "we shall split our forces. I shall take charge of one of the armies. As much as I don't crave to divide our power, it shall allow us to be more mobile. Also, dismiss the camp followers. If they stay, they stay at their own risk and peril."

"Who will lead the other force?" Lee asked. His face attempted to look nonchalant but it did not fool Washington who caught a hint of selfishness deep within Lee's eyes.

Lee's catastrophe at Monmouth was not forgotten or forgiven by Washington as well as other forbearances. Washington's face quickly turned red as he looked into Lee's eyes. "I shall hast none of your arrogance here. I know you eagerly took credit for the victory at Saratoga, e'en though you arrived at the end to claim the lion's share of the victory, although General Schuyler had done most of the planning, and Benedict Arnold and Daniel Morgan did the bleeding for you. You are a good general under decrees and direction and we need you. But this time the command will go to Lafayette."

Arnold could not help but smile at Washington's words but he held his tongue in cheek.

Lee rubbed his hands unconsciously. "*Le petite* French boy. Is that wise?"

Lafayette gave Lee a look of daggers. This name was whispered by those that disliked him but never spoken out loud.

Washington snapped, "It is done!" He walked over to Lafayette. "We have sent dispatches to Franklin in France. He was close to gaining military support in our war for independence. I have no doubt they will send military aid as soon as possible after hearing the tidings of our misfortune. I want you to personally visit the Oneida that came to our hour of want. I'm sure they can convince the entire Confederacy to help us. Ask them to help us. Also, they have the best scouts. They are gifted in hunting and tracking. Work with 'em to capture one of those creatures. These Reprobi, as I hear they call themselves. And try to learn more about this horsetail. What doth the Native's mean when they say they got it wrong?"

Washington turned to Arnold. "You will go with Lafayette and serve as his second in command. I need a man I can trust." A quick glance at Lee. "One who can follow orders. I know you will serve him well. You are an ardent patriot and a grizzled warrior. As further demonstrated recently by thy sacrifice at the broil of Saratoga. You refused amputation, content to hast a crippled left leg two inches shorter than your right."

Washington gently touched Muhlebnerg's shoulder. "Pastor, shalt you marshal'st us in prayer?"

Muhlenberg lowered his head. "Let us pray," he replied. "Would do your souls good to give your supplications to the Almighty." He pulled out his Bible from his coat and read, "To everything, there is a season, and a time to every purpose under the heaven: A time to be born, and a time to die; a time to plant, and a time to pluck up that which is planted; A time to kill, and a time to heal; a time to break down, and a time to build up; A time to weep, and a time to laugh; a time to mourn, and a time to dance; A time to cast away stones, and a time to gather stones together; a time to embrace, and a time to refrain from embracing; A time to get, and a time to lose; a time to keep, and a time to cast away; A time to rend, and a time to sew; a time to keep silence, and a time to speak; A time to love, and a time to hate; a time of war, and a time of peace." He cleared his throat. "And a time of war. On this occasion, the good shepherds must fight off predators to protect his flock. We fight for love and naught is stronger than that. Bow your heads."

Peter finished with the Lord's Prayer, and then they prayed with the men in the tent for the souls of their departed brothers to rest in peace in God's loving embrace and for God to deliver them victory over the Reprobi.

That evening, George Washington entered a quiet stable to seek solitude. On his knees alone with his sword on one side and his hat lying beside him, his hands clasped and raised to heaven to the almighty God, in vocal prayer he beseeched the Lord to interpose with divine aid to intervene with his mercy.

CHAPTER 18

VIVE LA LAFAYETTE

After the battle with the Reprobi, War Chief Shenandoah led his warriors to camp a short distance from Valley Forge. They were given plenty of extra tents to use. With the loss of thousands in battle, there was plenty to spare. Washington had split his army and had already moved out with half earlier that morning. The remaining force was commanded by Lafayette, who would be arriving at their camp shortly.

Shenandoah was seated on a wood stool dressed in full regalia waiting for Lafayette's arrival. He wore a traditional headdress, more a feathered cap, that had two feathers straight up and one down that differentiated the Oneida from other tribes of the confederacy, and a beautiful leather braided necklace that displayed large bear claws adorned his neck. More distinguishing than his regalia was his face. The lines on his face etched the story of a hard life for the great leader. His eyes were those of a man who had lost what he knew he must lose, but that the knowledge did not soften them.

Shenandoah was enjoying his pipe, directly across from his son Thomas. They both sat cross-legged on the ground across from each other. Thomas looked up at his father proudly. His father radiated confidence. He was exactly the leader his people needed at this time. He had the confidence to hold his people together, to prevent them from giving in to fear.

After a deep inhale, Shenandoah sent a puff of smoke into the air. The wisp floated through the air above them.

"Word has been sent to the clan mothers of the battle with instructions for Daniel to be watchful. I am confident Daniel will do a good job protecting our people."

"Daniel loves you and his people. I'm sure he will make you proud."

A knock was heard on a post outside the tent. A voice followed: "Lafayette has arrived!"

A small group of men wearing mostly Continental uniforms mixed in with a few French military ones stood in the center of camp. Shenandoah with Thomas by his side was directly across from Lafayette. It was easy to spot Lafayette in the group. He looked almost too young to shave, but he held an intensity in his brown eyes that showed intelligence well beyond his years.

Although still a teenager, a French aristocrat, Marquis de Lafayette somehow convinced the Continental Army to commission him as a major general less than a year ago, although he spoke little English and lacked any battle experience. Washington had grown weary of the French mercenaries who had been sailing across the Atlantic to join the American army. Although many were fine soldiers, some were troublemakers who had been driven from the French army. Some of them openly mocked the American military. Lafayette needed to prove himself.

His first military action was at the Battle of Brandywine, near Philadelphia, on September 11, 1777, where Lafayette was shot in the calf. He impressed Washington by bravely refusing treatment so that he could lead a successful retreat. Lafayette became a fiercely loyal aide to Washington and wanted nothing more than to prove his worth to him. This would be the first major command of Lafayette, who had barely turned twenty, handed to him by Washington.

In a thick French accent, the Marquis de Lafayette spoke to the assembly of natives that surrounded his men. "George Washington, commander of the Continental Army, would like to offer his praise to your people. Your warriors had repeatedly proven themselves as exceptional scouts, and superb fighters. The Oneidas and Tuscaroras have a particular claim to attention and kindness, for their perseverance and fidelity against the tyranny of the British." Lafayette paused for a moment and looked around the crowd, his deep brown eyes staring through them. "For myself, it is an honor to meet with you. I welcome your timely help with pleasure and call you friends. We have the most urgent needs of our friends. We seek your help to spread the tidings of the evil you hast seen and unite the Confederacy as one. Only together may we defeat this evil plague that is set upon our lands."

Chief Shenandoah approached Lafayette. Both men looked into each other's eyes, almost nose to nose, grateful for friendship but unsure of the future.

"Come, my friend, we'll discuss our friendship in private now," Shenandoah said. He shook Lafayette's hand. "Although I am the war chief of my people, I must tell you I shall want to take present counsel from the tribal elders and must send word to the clan mothers ere I compose a decision."

Shenandoah dismissed the crowd, then gave instructions to show Lafayette's men hospitality and for the tribe's warriors and sachems to gather with him at dusk. Lafayette followed him to Shenandoah's tent.

Thomas turned to leave. A tall muscular warrior blocked his path.

Han poked him with a finger. "We lost many brothers to help the colonists' army. 'Tis wise to continue helping them? We could all perish from what we now face. How can we even fight this evil? The horsetail was useless . . . useless as breasts on a bull."

Thomas frowned. "I was wrong about the horsetail. I was so sure of it. If you had only seen the conviction in Jacob's eyes as he drew his last breath."

"I receive you. Maybe he passed from this life ere he could give you more insight?"

Polly passed by in a rush and nearly tripped over Thomas. She stumbled but caught herself from falling down.

With one hand on her hip. "I'm not a lacrosse player to be knocked into, Thomas," she blurted out with a fiery look.

Thomas did his best not to grin but he failed and let one slip. "Polly, good to see you! 'Tis said you taught the men at Valley Forge how to prepare corn for eating."

Polly harrumphed. "They're like a lost tribe, these Europeans, yet they seem to somehow aye advance on us. This I will never understand."

Han nodded in agreement. "They may be babes, yet they know how to bite and sting. They've done a lot of damage to us over the years. They encroached on our lands. We are closer to their ways now than our ancestors. Oh, how the great peacemaker would role i' his grave."

"Rollover in his grave indeed," Polly said. "Our men begin to forget in every decision, we must consider the impact of our decisions on the next generation. You're stubborn like an ass." She bit her lower lip in frustration. "Mothers carry a child from birth. Mothers nurse and care for a child in every way so that the infant knows the hands that held them are a dependable love. All men, no matter what country they are fighting for, they all have mothers, and mothers don't send their sons out to kill other mothers' sons. The peace in the Confederacy was secured at Onondaga Lake, where they planted a Tree of Peace and proclaimed the Laws of the Confederacy. A peace that needed to be kept." Her shoulders slumped and her voice faltered. "The great Peacemaker said we should all love one another and live together in peace. If we fail him it will only lead to disaster. We are close now to destruction. We must unite the Confederacy to help protect us from any further harm."

Han and Thomas glanced at each other, then back at Polly, unsure what to say for the moment after hearing such deep emotion carried on her words.

Han broke the silence.

"You're right," he said. "I did not intend to kill other mothers' sons when I was put on this earth. These creatures that we fought, however . . . are not born of a woman. They must be destroyed!"

"I am in agreement with Han," Thomas said. "Whatever bore these creatures—if anything—must have been lacking in goodness. They are evil incarnate, and as such, I believe the great Peacemaker would want us to smite them before the earth plunges into darkness."

Polly tugged one of her braids. "I agree these creatures are evil and should be destroyed," she said. "Once you have smitten them, however, I fear that our people will not return to the love and peace as the great Peacemaker would want for us."

Polly frowned then slowly walked away. Thomas made a move to follow. Han placed his hand on Thomas's shoulder.

"Let her be," Han said. "It is best to leave her be when she is in this mood. She does not let others take any burdens that she carries. And her burden is a great weight. She carries the worries of our nation upon her shoulders. She shall make our people proud one day as a clan mother."

At dusk, Thomas and Han were the first to arrive to listen to their war chief's address to his people. The largest wooden cabin built at Valley Forge was offered for the meeting. Plenty of candles cast a flickering light, more than enough to illuminate the inside. The building originally used to house fifty men was overcrowded with every warrior fit to fight and Sachem that could squeeze in. They sat shoulder to shoulder. Combined body heat was enough for sweat to trickle down everyone's face as they waited for Shenandoah to arrive. Those that could not fit within sat outside the open door sitting on the ground in silence.

Chief Shenandoah took a seat in front of the crowd. He wasted no time addressing the assembly: "Washington has asked for every able-bodied man to fight this evil. Lafayette has given us belts and gold coins as friendship inducements and has agreed to hand over all the cannon at Fort Schuyler to protect our nation, although I believe we are safe from imminent attack. The British hast bigger prey to hunt. I am confident they shall join with the colonists' army. Our enemies in the Confederacy shall forbear any incursions. We have sent envoys and we are waiting for their return. I believe the Confederacy shall be united quickly. Lafayette hath promised us we shall serve under French instead of colonial patriot commanders would we crave this. He receives the French shall send forces soon. I have chosen to accept their offer. This offer is better than those who have one foot in the canoe, and one foot in the boat, going to fall into the river. The council of elders hast agreed and I'm sure the clan mothers will agree. A message of our agreement has been sent to them. We should'st grant all we can. I believe if we give all we can grant besides saving ourselves from this evil among our mist the colonists shall forever be in debt to us, and this will help secure a lasting peace with them." Chief Shenandoah drew himself up. "It is settled."

The next morning the sound of beating drums was heard. Lafayette and his delegation, with a few others, joined in celebration with the natives. A wide space just outside the defensive fortifications of the Valley Forge encampment was used.

The drums beat for a round dance, also known as the friendship dance, to begin. The music pulled at the Native American hearts with every beat to the rhythm. Soon, the beat changed and the dancing began. The dancers moved in a circular pattern in a clockwise direction stepping and swinging arms to the hard and soft beat. Thomas led the dancers to coil up like a snake and then uncoiled. As the dancers passed in front of one another, they gave greetings, joy, and laughter.

Lafayette with his entourage joined in the fun, joining the dancers. The natives laughed at the attempt. Lafayette lost his footing then slipped hitting the ground face first. As he was losing his footing, he accidentally stuck his foot out just enough for Polly Cooper to catch it and fall to her knees.

As Polly brushed off the dirt from her dress and stood up there was a momentary flare of anger in her face. She whipped her head around hard then stared at Lafayette.

"I'm not a soldier to be knocked into," she blurted out in her native tongue.

Lafayette's face grew red with embarrassment as he pondered what she said to him.

"I am sorry for my clumsiness," he said. "The dance is more difficult than it looks." He gave a polite smile.

"Maybe you shouldn't dance?" replied Polly in broken English.

Lafayette paused in thought then replied. He spoke slowly so she would understand his words. "None is born a dancer. Dancing with the feet is one thing. Dancing with the heart is another. Just because people can't dance, doesn't mean they should'st not dance."

Polly must have been pleased with his answer. She tried to maintain a smooth face, but the beginnings of a grin made her cheeks seem even plumper. To avoid smiling she jumped back into the dance.

The alliance with the Native Americans was sealed. The tribes of the Hausdensee, who sided with the colonists initially, and most likely those that did not would join with Washington against the Reprobi. A partnership is strong but a trifecta is more powerful. Next, the Americans needed to seal an official alliance with the British. The recent battle with the Reprobi was one thing but a formal alliance was another. With the recent bloodshed between the two and complications of combining military forces, it would not prove easy but was necessary if the Sons of Adam wanted to survive the rise of the Reprobi.

CHAPTER 19

TO CATCH A SNAKE

Utilizing a series of carved-out wooden bunkers below the earth, the Reprobi camp was well hidden. Every possible precaution was taken to hide from the Sons of Adam. The campfire flames remained invisible and with the use of airway tunnels, the fire burned so hotly that it reduced the smoke output. Camouflage netting made from strips of cloth with leaves and twigs tied to them helped cover the entrances to avoid detection. In addition to camp alterations, a few of Lucivia's scouts acted as lookouts to make sure the humans did not venture too close.

Mikmash sensed the air, collecting chemical signatures from his flickering tongue. The smallest particle could warn if any human was approaching the Reprobi campsite within a half-mile . . . that is if he continued to be a vigilant sentry. After a few hours, he thumbed his claws into an old hickory tree out of boredom. The words 'We need no God!' were cut into the tree. He removed his helmet, adorned with a large spike from a prehistoric rhino long buried in the earth. It still held dry human bloodstains from battle. His eyes continued to grow heavy until he slumped against the tree breathing heavily out his nostrils.

Mikmash dreamed. The sun shone brilliantly out of a cloudless blue sky. Sharp bolts of lightning struck through the air in brilliant flashes as thunder boomed. He watched with his brothers as Lucifer sat on an ornate carved wooden chair on top of a pile of human heads set in anguished faces. He drummed his claws on the armrests with a long wicked smile on his face.

Thunderous applause and hollers were thrown at him. The voices raised to a deafening crescendo. Lucifer raised a hand and the voices immediately stopped. He rose from his chair.

He looked upon his brothers lovingly. "My brothers," he said, "you will receive all that was promised and more! What the holy father would not give to us, we have taken by force! We partner with him now as equals!"

The Reprobi collectively bowed to their Lord.

In a blink, Mikmash was sitting on a gilded gold throne. His body transformed to his true form, that of a beautiful angel. A fresh-cut garland of flowers served as his crown. As lord of his domain, he was dressed as he pleased. He wore a fine but rather simple white robe. In contrast, his human chattels attending him were entirely in the nude, with their eyes held in blind servitude. He turned towards a servant bringing him a sup of wine. *You do what you were designed to do. God has created us to serve and worship him; you have been made to serve and worship us.* He smiled.

A crack of a branch woke Mikmash. He twisted his snake-like head toward the sound. An arrow had shot into his hand, sticking him to the tree. He looked at the arrow shaft with his eyes wide. He howled in rage.

Out of the shadows of the trees, Han sprinted towards him. With a motion, Mikmash pulled his hand free with the arrow still sticking through it. He glanced at his battle-axe, which for him was regrettably a few steps away. He pulled out his dagger, a wicked 18-inch blade he named Muciviaton, translated from the first language as "Blaze." Han dodged the blade, and then kicked it out of Mikmash's hand.

Mikmash bent over to retrieve the blade. With a sharp kick to the head, Mikmash went down. Followed by a series of brutal kicks, most to the head, Mikmash was knocked unconscious.

A small band of Native Americans approached. They numbered 10. Mikmash was immediately gagged then tied, hand and foot. He was searched and stripped of any belongings. They removed his iron ring armor and left only his pteruges on, a defensive skirt of multiple layered pieces of leather. They took his axe and dagger. Mikmash was attached to a pole and hoisted upon the shoulders of four hunters. They quickly moved the heavy burden.

After a mile with sweat glistening on his brow, Han heard the sound of hoofbeats approaching. They hid Mikmash in the brush and notched arrows.

Lafayette and a small party of eight were seen approaching on horseback. They were heavily armed. Multiple rifles were tied to each saddle. They brought with them a large muscular draft horse with no rider.

Han drew himself out of cover then walked up to Lafayette who came to a stop.

Han smiled as he patted Lafayette's horse. "We have captured one of them."

"This is marvelous!" Lafayette said. "We are blessed to hast your help. Your people are truly amazing trackers and hunters. Much better than the prey you sought. What you have accomplished today will be talked about for many generations."

Han's face was unmoving. "There is no need for praise. We did what needed to be done. For this, I am content enough."

The Reprobi was hoisted out of the brush and brought to Lafayette.

"Dear Lord!" Lafayette exclaimed. "Its eyes are just like ours. These creatures look like a blend, a 'twixt of snake and a man. I wonder if this was the creature that convinced Eve to eat the forbidden fruit in Paradise?"

Han shook his head. "I cannot tell you this. I was not there. Perhaps we should be continuing on the plan."

"Indeed. Let's scurry this creature away, shall we?"

The prisoner was placed over a draft horse like a large sack of potatoes. The party encircled the draft horse that now carried a rider. The party dug their heels into the horse's flanks then rode off tearing the earth in their tracks.

Han and the natives watched Lafayette ride off. They were pleased. Not so much as relief from carrying the foul creature but that they had removed an abomination that did not belong to their land. Mother Earth had not given birth to this creature. These creatures disturbed the balance and purity of the blessed earth. There was no question the Reprobi had to be removed.

The prisoner was taken on a day's march to a gap hidden deep in the Appalachian Mountains. The location was far away from any civilization with deep forest overhead. A small cave with barely enough room to hold the large prisoner was at the center of a small camp made up of a Continental company commanded by Captain Nathaniel Chapman. Iron bars previously removed from a cell were transported and installed at the cave entrance. The prisoner was ungagged, untied, then pushed in. The gate was securely locked then a guard posted a few steps away.

With the prisoner safely secured Lafayette departed to return to Washington.

Once inside Mikmash stood up. Every muscle in his body remained perfectly still and quiet. The only sound unheard was his mind racing with thoughts of escape and anger. So much anger he needed to exhale. He boiled anger, preparing to unleash it when the moment presented itself. He hoped it would be soon.

After a few minutes, Nathaniel approached. He looked at the Reprobi intent to decipher his mysteries. "How is the prisoner?" Nathaniel asked the guard. He knew him as George Paine, one of the sergeants in his company, a lean man, bald with a couple of days of facial growth.

George shrugged. "He has not moved at all. Only to breathe as far as I can tell."

"Strange, it is so quiet. They were surely factious when they chopped us down at Monmouth."

"They surely did but we survived and that's all that matters. Brick by brick, instant by instant, we live through another day."

The guard absently took a step back towards the cell bars.

A reptilian arm reached out its claws and swiped the back of his neck. The cut was deep, almost decapitating him. He gurgled for a moment as blood poured out from his severed jugular vein. His body collapsed in a heap.

"I thank you for this morning's exercise," sneered Mikmash. His face contorted in a fang-twisted wry grin.

Nathaniel's face turned white, then slowly turned red with rage. He took a step closer to the cell. He stared at the Reprobi with murder in his eyes. He took a deep breath then began to control his emotions, unlike his rapid heartbeat that was not stopping. He shook his head then bent over to pull the body away.

"Fetch yourselves!" Nathaniel called out. He was immediately answered by two men who gaped eyes wide as they looked at the corpse.

"Wha—Wha—happened?" one of them exclaimed.

"Dead!" Nathaniel said flatly. "Please take the body. I will finish George's watch."

The body was removed then Nathaniel turned his attention to the Reprobi. He studied the creature. He noticed its hand. *Didn't they say an arrow stuck through and impaled the creature's hand on a tree? Yet no wound is visible. I wonder.*

Nathaniel gave Mickmash an icy stare. "I see you recovered quickly from the arrow. 'Tis said your kind heals quickly. I desire to learn how this is."

Mikmash grasped the bars. "We heal because we are immortal, while your kind, the Sons of Adam, is weak."

Nathaniel took a step towards the cell, careful not to be in the range of Mikmash's quick arms. "Weak you say," he said. "Are you not held by these iron bars while I stand here?"

Mikmash's face contorted as he strained his muscles pulling at the bars. The bars held fast in the stone. Rage compelled him, knowing the human was absolutely right in this situation. He lowered his eyes in defeat preparing to release the bars.

In a flash of movement Nathaniel, with a knife hidden in his belt, sliced a finger off. The hand squirted red blood as the finger dropped to the ground.

Mikmash's eyes that were already red seemed to be set ablaze. He picked up the finger and threw it at Nathaniel.

Nathaniel caught the finger with his hand.

"Let's just see how long your hand takes to heal," Nathaniel said.

CHAPTER 20

A MOST CAPTIVATING PRISONER

Captain Nathaniel Chapman was personally selected by Lafayette to take charge of the captured Reprobi and to extract any useful information from it. Nathaniel had proven his leadership on the battlefield. He held the line where lesser men would have fled in terror. Lafayette hoped Nathaniel's strength of will would get the answers out of the Reprobi. Perhaps discover a weakness. Washington was counting on success. In fact, delivered answers from the Reprobi could yield valuable insight into humanity's very survival.

Nathaniel was up at dawn delivering another report to Lafayette. After three uneventful days, the Reprobi prisoner, Mikmash, it called itself, refused to say anything valuable. They found conversing with Mikmash was like dealing with a slick salesperson. Mixing words with the Reprobi twisted your mind, making it difficult to think straight. The delivered report said very little.

Nathaniel returned on horseback to his base camp along a trail covered overhead by a thick forest canopy. The fog of fatigue still lingered in his head. It could be remedied with coffee at camp but first, he wanted to talk with his prisoner some more. Perhaps this time he would unravel something useful.

Fearing recapture of their prisoner, Nathaniel had the Reprobi moved deep within a nearby cave. A metal cage previously used to transport prisoners to the gallows was fixed carefully inside to contain their dangerous captive.

Nathaniel rode through camp, which consisted of two tentfuls of men, on a white-footed chestnut horse. He chose the best; the remainder of his company he left under the charge of Lieutenant Ethan Davis and Sergeant Abner Smith.

He approached the hidden cave entrance just outside of camp. He slowly loosened his grip on his reins. A slice of hell waited inside the dark entrance. Sharp thoughts came to mind. *Why me! Surely what they need is a philosopher. I did prove they heal fast. Its finger has already grown back with the claw just beginning to reappear. That was easy. But through conversation with it? When it speaks it is only to attempt to cast doubt in our minds. A weak mind would easily succumb to its will of words.*

With a long neigh, the horse was stopped outside the cave entrance. Its eyes looked as if it wanted to bolt. Nathaniel patted the horse on the neck.

"Good morning, sir," the guard at the entrance said. He clicked the butt of his rifle on the ground then saluted. Private Samuel Morris did not wear his tricorn hat. The hat had been lost in the escape at Monmouth and not yet been replaced. His long locks of brown hair could use a good pass of a brush. Bags under his eyes showed a lack of sleep on his face but alertness was fixed deep within his eyes. He knew as did all of the men the importance of his duty and their mission.

"Good morning, Samuel. How is our guest today?" Nathaniel came down from his horse and tied the mare to a nearby tree.

"It's a primrose office, sir. This creature doesn't stir nor e'en move."

"Let's hope this creature will stir us some answers today," Nathaniel said.

Samuel knelt down. He took a piece of flint stone in his left hand. With his steel knife, he struck it hard. A small glowing ember fell off on a small piece of hemp char cloth that was tightly pressed against the stone. It quickly glowed red. One of several candles lying nearby was lit. "Here, sir," he said as he handed Nathaniel the candle.

Nathaniel nodded appreciatively then took the candle. He stared at the cave entrance. He shook his head in thought. *This time you're going to give me something I can use.*

Inside the cave, a bead of moisture rolled down the stone crack then dripped onto the head of Mikmash. He sat cross-legged, head down, pretending to sleep. He wanted to give the impression he was oblivious to his confinement. His presence was anything but oblivious. To his guards, he was evil incarnate. A representation of sin punished. They did not understand the meaning of the Reprobi yet, but they knew they were to be feared.

Nathaniel entered the cave. A horrible odor struck him like a serpent's rotting carcass. Hand-wrought heavy iron oil lamps hung on long iron nails stuck in the walls. He used his candle to light the lamps. They cast a flickering glow on the rock walls. He approached the back of the cave moving in silence, hearing only his thoughts. *The bars will hold, right?* Nathaniel's heartbeat began to quicken. *The bars are thick. Just don't get too close to them.*

On the cave floor next to the cage lay a torch. He lifted it up then lit it with his candle. A wisp of smoke blew as he snuffed the candle out, using his fingers on the wick.

He looked into the cage, shining torchlight onto Mikmash. The mix of snake and man raised its head with a jerk. Its human eyes opened then its mouth gave a twisted smile.

"Greetingsss, my friend," Mikmash said. "I have missed our conversation. I have not told you anything valuable. Of this, I am sure. But this I will tell you. This I will promise you. Release me. Beyond letting you live; I will give you all the delights you treasure. I will give you everything your heart desiresss. I see you as an officer. How unfortunate, such a low rank. How would you like to command an army as a general, or even better, rule your own personal kingdom? I have the authority to make this happen. All you have to do is set me free. I promise you!"

Sharp visions flashed in Nathaniel's head. Visions of himself sitting on a large throne with an oversized jewel-encrusted crown on his head. The crown slipped off.

I have no need for wealth, he thought to himself. *Although my wife is dead I hast my children to return to and they are worth more to me than streets paved with gold. I shall return to 'em, won't I?*

"I imagine you're barking up the wrong tree," Nathaniel said. "It's not the earthly rewards I desire."

"Then what is it you desire? You only have to ask for it then I will make it so."

"If you don't know, I'm not going to tell you."

Mikmash visibly shuttered with disappointment.

"Release me!" Mikmash looked deeply into Nathaniel's eyes. "If you do not I can see that you suffer. You will endure agony for all eternity!"

Nathaniel shook his head. *Lies, lies. Receive never a word he says.*

"We have translated the word Reprobi as 'the fallen,' Nathaniel said. "Maybe a better word is Reprobi Angeli for 'fallen angels.' You are evil. Your hideous appearance reflects the nature that God suffered you to hast."

"Evil! What do you know about evil?" Mikmash said. "Ha!" He spit on the ground. "You think a snake is a manifestation of evil. Because of its appearance, you condemn it. If you ask my opinion, the Sons of Adam are very ugly. Looks can be deceptive. We were not always like this. We were once beautiful. We still are beautiful on the inside. It is in the heart that beauty truly lies. This appearance is meaningless. It is only temporary, like sand through an hourglass. God cast us out and he gave us this appearance as punishment, we who are innocent. Our only crime was that Lucifer stood for us. We will be beautiful again. As for representing evil, my people represent the good. Lucifer is not evil. You are the evil ones if you continue doing God's bidding."

"Your kind represents the good . . . methinks not," said Pastor and General Peter Muhlenberg. Nathaniel nearly jolted with surprise hearing the voice of his compatriot.

Peter stared at the Reprobi with a look of disgust. Peter was a square fellow with heavy eyebrows that always seemed drawn in thought. He was known to have cast off his minister robes for command at the onset of the Revolution to the chagrin of his family until his brother Fredrick, who was also a minister, changed his tune and joined himself when the British burned down his own church in front of him.

"Sorry, General, I didn't see you approach," Nathaniel said. He shook the General's hand. Although Peter outranked him, Nathaniel was in charge of the mission.

"No bother, Captain. I know 'tis hard to focus with its evil presence. I myself can only stand for a short time due to the anxiety this creature causes me. I had a good night's sleep. I figured I'd hast another go with it today."

"Well, isn't it the good pastor," Mikmash hissed. "Thinking of preaching to me some more? To a being that has lived since the dawn of creation and has witnessed heaven with his own eyes. A place that you have never seen but have only dreamed of."

"You were cast out from heaven; you spawn of Satan!" Muhlenberg bellowed.

Mikmash scratched his claws on the cage. The metal sent shivers down the men's spines.

"Oh, cast out from heaven for sure," Mikmash sneered. "And, yes, we are transformed. We don't ever deny God is the father and creature of us all, but I tell you the truth, he is the great deceiver. He is the evil one. He doesn't love you. He threw us out for having our own thoughts. He threw you out of Paradise for the same."

Muhlenberg's face grew red. His voice quivered with emotion. "We are descendants of Adam blessed in God's own image. God is good. He loves us."

"God is good?" Mikmash's red eyes twinkled with enjoyment. "You have been deceived. Adam was a pet created for amusement only and Eve a plaything for Adam. Both pets were created for entertainment. Lucifer sees this. He doesn't want you as pets. He wants to set you free. Free that you can escape the bondage of slavery and servitude. To give you joy. Think for a moment, why does God need to be worshipped?"

"It is not that he needs worship," Muhlenberg said. "By worshipping him, we give glory to the One who deserves our worship. He wants us to love Him. Through loving Him and because of salvation from Jesus we can go home to Him when we leave this earth. It is through Him our Father that eternal destiny depends upon."

"Ha!" Mikmash cackled. He squeezed the metal bar of his cage. Ripped muscles were visible on his black reptilian arms. He stared at Muhlenberg as if Muhlenberg were a lost lamb. "We worshipped God as our father. Look at what happened to us! We who were innocent! He cannot be trusted to dispense justice. Look at your race. Eve ate the forbidden fruit. Such a simple thing, yet your descendants are punished for eternity. You have it all wrong. Your destiny depends on his whim. Your salvation is through us."

Nathaniel's hand pressed on his forehead. *Talking with this creature is like talking to a brick wall.* His head pain told him it was time to rest someplace quiet, to clear his thoughts. He would go for his cup of coffee and check on his men.

"General, if you will forgive me," he said. "I must take my leave. Please continue with my absence"

"Please take your deliverance." Muhlenberg squinted at Mikmash. "Fish and unwanted guests stink after a few hours."

Mikmash visibly relaxed then sat on the floor cross-legged. He used his claw to sketch an image on the dirt floor. Muhlenberg watched Mikmash work curiously in silence. The image became recognizable, two poorly drawn figures, one a Reprobi and one human both holding hands.

Mikmash looked up at his captor. "Love is not a want, it is a need," he said. "The need for love is what makes the both of us separate from God's other creationsss. There are many types of love. The most common form is friendship love. In this love, two people follow the rule of you for yourself, I for myself, however, we will have no expectations in the relationship. The strongest form of love sits on a foundation of bedrock. It transcends all conventions of mutual expectations, being founded on the rule, I am for you, you're for whoever you choose; I settle for your wishes with no expectations in the relationship. The Reprobi offer this strongest form of love to you." He attempted to make his face look soothing and peaceful but it was impossible with his snakelike face. "Will you take it?"

Muhlenberg looked up with an expression of thought. "Hmmm . . . methinks not from the likes of you."

In an instant, Mikmash gripped the bars. His red eyes locked on Muhlenberg as if he would go through his cage and pull Muhlenberg apart, limb from limb. Mikmash gritted his teeth, angry with himself for failing to persuade the Sons of Adam to the truth as he saw it. This pastor he had to agree was a worthy opponent in mind chess. But he thought there would be weaker ones. Those he could convert.

"Begone from me, preacher, and take your lies with you!" *Bring me, someone I can influence*, he thought. "You will learn the truth! The truth is eternal and will never change!"

In defeat, Mikmash returned to ignoring the humans. His body remained limp but his mind boiled with thoughts of how to manipulate the Sons of Adam. He needed to escape. He was confident he would. It would only be a question of when.

CHAPTER 21

DREAM WALKER

There are two types of dreams, those that are clearly imagined and those so real that one cannot separate them from reality. This dream was the latter. Nathaniel approached his home. The log cabin was how he remembered it, its worn wooden front door slightly ajar after slipping slightly from its bracket.

He swung the door wide open. Elizabeth sat on a short stool working her flywheel spinning thread into thick yarn that twisted on the bobbin in her hand. Her presence there took his breath away. She was everything he remembered. Her bonnet was off, displaying flowing dirt-blond hair. Her green emerald eyes held pools of perpetual light that reflected his love.

She glimpsed Nathaniel. She dropped her bobbin then ran to Nathaniel. Elizabeth hugged him gently, then harder until his ribs hurt. She released him after a kiss on his lips.

Nathaniel's jaw dropped. "Elizabeth, I thought you w-were . . . de-ead?"

"What silliness is this?" She held a finger to her lip. "Ssshhh, dear. You will wake the baby. I can assure you I'm quite alive." She chuckled.

"And there is someone that wants to see you. Your new son." She motioned to a crib beside her. A beautiful baby boy lay in the crib. It cooed and gurgled softly.

"But how did . . . ? He was . . . childbirth? You both?"

Elizabeth held his hand then led him to sit on the stool she had sat on before. Her hands remained on his, applying soft pressure. Her soft face hardened to seriousness as she stared into his eyes.

"Dear, I know that you love us. I wonder what you would sacrifice if I had died. What would you do for us to return to you?"

She kissed him.

"I would be willing to give my life," he answered.

"Truly?"

Another kiss.

"Yes!"

"You do not have to go that far, my husband. All you need to do is let Mikmash go."

"What? Mikmash?" Nathaniel croaked.

"The good creature you have in your prison. Do you remember his promises? I can be returned to you along with our child. We can live like royalty!"

As the last word was uttered, Nathaniel's heart sank. Any delusion that this was real was over. He looked up at her fevered eyes. *My heart beat again to believe. But she is truly dead.*

"I do not care to live like royalty," he snapped.

The dream world immediately turned cloudy, but the image of Elizabeth remained vivid. A picture of comeliness as she picked up the baby and held it to her bosom.

"My love, do not let me go!" Elizabeth beckoned. "I fear the darkness. Our family can have it all. It would be easy for you. You run the camp. You can make it look like an accident. No one will get hurt. Maybe the key . . ."

Nathaniel's face grew tight. His eyes narrowed. Anger began to boil inside. He turned away from Elizabeth. "You are not my wife! My wife is dead and so is my child!"

When Nathaniel peeked at Elizabeth her form changed into a man dressed in a Continental uniform with no rank or insignia.

The man spoke: "No more games. I know you love your wife. You are in pain for her. Why hurt? Why ever hurt again? I will be direct: Let Mikmash go, and your wife and child will be returned to you immediately. Deny me, and I will make sure they burn in hell for all eternity. The choice is yours."

The image of the soldier faded to be replaced by the image of Mikmash, albeit dressed in the same Continental uniform. This time there was a rank insignia, one star on a golden epaulet giving him the rank of general.

"Your persuasion is bootless. How could I ever know that you speak the truth?" Nathaniel said.

"You do not trust me? One of your own soldiers?" Mikmash hissed. His clawed finger gently tapped his chest. "Surely, we have fought alongside each other, have we not?"

Nathaniel harrumphed. "What are you talking about? We have never fought together. It is insulting seeing you in this uniform. You wear the clothes of one of my soldiers, but deep down inside, your heart—if you have one—is lacking love and the support of God."

Mikmash shrugged. "You seem so sure of this? How can you be so sure that the one you call 'God' is not against you? Was it not he who damned all of mankind after Eve had eaten the forbidden fruit in the Garden of Eden? And did he not burn the citizens of Sodom and Gomorrah for crimes they had committed, and also in the process turn Lot's wife into salt for the mere act of looking back? Surely, you also remember that he left Moses and the rest of the Jews to be slaves to the Egyptians for many years."

Nathaniel crossed his arms. "It was your kind who tempted Eve to eat the forbidden fruit, and who so irredeemably corrupted the citizens of Sodom and Gomorrah that God had no choice but to burn them. As for Moses and the Jews, you also forget that one day, they rose up, with God smiting every first-born Egyptian child, just as we will rise up against you and send you back to the pit you crawled out of."

The eyes of Mikmash turned a fiery red. "My patience runs thin, Ssson of Adam. Fortunately for you, I am merciful, and I offer you a final chance to think this over. Allow me to escape and your wife and son will be returned to you! If not they will suffer in the pit that you call hell!"

An image of Elizabeth and his newborn flashed in his mind. They beckoned with loving eyes asking for his love. A bright white fire appeared, engulfing them. Elizabeth and the baby screamed in agony. He watched their skin bubble and catch fire like dried paper.

Tears rolled down Nathaniel's eyes. *This is not real!* he thought. *This is a dream!* Awake! He closed then opened his eyes. They still burned. The fire ended with blackened corpses now smoldering.

Nathaniel's mind raced, caught in a thinking conundrum. *What if it is speaking the truth? What should I do?* His thoughts drifted to the words of Benjamin Franklin, who spoke of a simple decision-making tool. *Make a positive and negative checklist. The one with the most underneath it is the winner.* He easily filled the negative list. At the forefront of that list was the release of Mikmash could possibly change the outcome of the war with the Reprobi. He went to the positive list. Other than his own happiness, it would be empty. *She is already gone. Wherever she is, she feels no pain. She is in God's embrace. We are here for a short while anyway. I can wait for her. My time will be only a blink. I must take care of the rest of my family ere I depart this world.*

Nathaniel released his clenched teeth with a heat-filled voice. "No!"

Nathaniel grabbed Mikmash's arm. He held his clawed hand as he swung his arm back to give a punch. The dream world images were now a blur. He punched. The dream ended abruptly.

He awoke, soaked in sweat. Getting up he splashed some cold water on his face, changed his cotton shirt, and then returned to his cart. *Was it a dream?* he thought. *Can the Reprobi enter them?* He closed his eyes, trying to think of images that would give happiness and joy. He drifted off to natural sleep. No sweet dreams came, only nightmares.

CHAPTER 22

ESCAPE

The calm chirping sound of crickets resounded just as the sun went below the horizon. Light and crisp air blew, helping make the perfect temperature to get comfortable. The guard's eyes began to nod. He shook his head, attempting to fight off the drowsiness with its persistent attack, but his defense could not defeat the symphony of tranquility nor his musket resting over his lap. His eyes closed and from his chest came the first guttural snore.

The sound of snoring floated through the airways and found its way into the dark cave. The only light in the cell was the red glow of Mikmash's eyes that opened at the sound. He cackled softly to himself just before his form began to skip into a misty cloud. It floated through the cave, pausing at the guard. As the man breathed the mist went into his nostrils.

Finally, Mikmash thought to himself. *At sleep, the Son of Adam is at its weakest.* Mikmash stood up in human form then he looked down to his left then right examining his new body. He placed the musket over his shoulder with its strap. Nothing else interested him, with the exception of a knife with a handle made from a deer antler. He pulled out the knife and studied it. He poked his arm to test the sharpness. A bead of blood formed.

Sharp enough for these creatures to shave with. He licked his teeth with his tongue. *A little fun before I go back to my body.*

Silent as death, he ran.

Nathaniel was startled by a shadowy figure that ran through his tent. He glanced to where his sword leaned against the wall. The figure shook him.

"Captain! Captain!"

Nathaniel recognized the soldier as Jacob. A tough fellow even though he looked so thin a strong breeze could knock him over.

Nathaniel sat up. "What is it, Jacob?" He yawned.

"I went to relieve the guard, only I did not find him nor the prisoner," Jacob stuttered.

"What the shite! Sound the alarm, gather everyone!"

Jacob flew out of the tent.

Nathaniel dressed quickly, tying his saber to his belt. The last touch was his tricorn hat.

"Captain!"

"Yes, Jacob?"

Nathaniel caught the face of Jacob in the pale morning light. He looked pale as if he has just seen a ghost.

"Jacob, what is it?"

"Captain, I went to fetch the men. One tent is full; they're mustered outside. As for the other tents . . . they won't be joining us on account their throats have all been cut."

Nathaniel rushed out of the tent, pushing Jacob aside. He drew his saber. The sound of thunder rumbled across the sunrise, calling for a storm coming. A line of a dozen men with faces that looked confused and anguished stood at attention. Muhlenberg stood to their side looking up mumbling in prayer.

"Men, it is urgent we do not fail. This creature . . . this demon . . . this Reprobi . . . whatever you bid to call it is valuable, valuable beyond what you can ever fathom. It must be captured whatever the price. You all have been selected for this assignment because of your skills and bravery on the battlefield. We pursue it now in earnest. And if it is to our deaths, so be it!"

A few sprinkles of rain were heard, hitting the tree leaves, and then the sprinkles became a downpour.

"Let's move out!"

They quickly became drenched to the bone as they chased for the Reprobi's trail. Nathaniel did his best to puzzle out his thoughts. *How didst the Reprobi escape? Maybe the guard felt an itch to check towards the Reprobi and was tricked to free it. For some, warrants can pull at the heart. There shall need to be a better screening of guards if we can capture the prisoner again.*

The skilled scouts in the group easily followed the man's trial, but they found no sign of the creature.

A sound came from the brush, barely audible over the rain. All paused, knelt, then cocked their firearms. Nathaniel drew his sword from his scabbard.

A wild turkey with a large black feathered body waddled out of the vegetation. It moved without fear. The bird's head was ugly but its presence emulated beauty and majesty. The words of Mikmash echoed in Nathaniel's mind. *We still are beautiful on the inside. It is in the heart that beauty lies.*

Mikmash made his way back to the Reprobi camp. He followed a deer trail headed towards the direction. He heard a gentle flow of water as he continued. The earth became soft, and he began to trudge through mud. He slipped and grabbed a clump of horsetail reed, a bamboo-like, vertical stem that seemed almost tropical in appearance. A tingling sensation rippled through his hand. With a whisp, he turned to a cloud of mist almost instantly then it blinked out.

The smell announced first what the search party was looking for. The guard's limbs had been hacked off its torso. The torso was tied to a tree with a knife stuck into his heart. Nathaniel approached the guard. His eyes met with the guard's lifeless eyes.

"This is not a way for a man to die."

Nathaniel used his hand to shut the eyelids gently. He pulled out the bone-handled knife stuck into the corpse. Blood dripped off the handle.

Nathaniel closed his eyes. His voice faltered, "Bury him."

The exhausted group returned to camp, drenched and feeling thoroughly defeated. Before changing into dry clothes, Nathaniel hopped on his horse then set out for Lafayette. He would deliver the news in person. The Reprobi had escaped and the detail attached to guard the prize failed. Washington would not be pleased.

CHAPTER 23

ACHILLES HEEL

The cold air of hell was broken by hot flames flickering inside many furnaces. Plenty of wood collected from above stoked the flames. Glowing orange metal was removed from them then placed on anvils. Day and night they were hammered into usable weapons and armour. Every Reprobi would be equipped for battle before the entire Legion marched out. They worked quickly. Although they had waited a plethora of years. Their time was now for the rise of the Reprobi.

One piece of weaponry could not be hammered by a smith. The Reprobi in battle witnessed the Sons of Adams carry flags into battle. A Reprobi standard was created to strike fear when they marched again. The cloth was spun from moth cocoons. It was dyed a bright red using carminic acid from crushed bugs found in the earth. A golden snake, dyed yellow from earth roots, was placed in the center. The snake body was vertical in position with its face appearing about to strike. An assortment of feathers collected from the surface formed large wings stitched to the left and right sides of it.

The most powerful weapon prepared to be deployed was Lucifer himself. His presence would serve as manna for their souls. Their love for their Lord, guardian, and protector was immeasurable. They believed Lucifer, favored in God's eyes, rebelled against the creator out of love for his brothers to preserve the truth and their freedom of will.

A water droplet fell onto Lucifer's head, disturbing the silence. Lucifer shook his head, flicking the wetness from his head. He drummed his fingers on the rough-cut arms of his throne. He was not bored; in fact, he was overwhelmed. Thoughts and visions raced in his mind. The uncertainty of the future frustrated him. With their escape from the earth, the door to the future was wide open, he was sure of it, and the Reprobi would write it.

Rexus ignored the guards at the entrance who saluted him with fists to their chest. He approached the throne then prostrated himself before Lucifer.

"Rise my brother," Lucifer said. "It pleases me to know that Eve ate the forbidden fruit. It shows that they can be led to the truth. We will bend them to our will but first, we must conquer them. How are the new weapons coming along?"

Rexus rose. "My Lord, we have not made much progressss. I feel it is best to capture more of the Sons of Adam to teach us about these weapons. At this time, we can only reproduce the metal balls they fire. We have a store of rifles, gunpowder, and ammunition removed from bodies off the field. We have begun practicing firing these weapons. I believe we can field a unit of 100. Each Legionnaire assigned will be able to fire about a dozen times till they are out of ammunition."

Lucifer gasped. "I see—"

A sudden bright flash of light appeared in front of the throne beside Rexus. Lucifer shrunk back against his throne shielding his eyes with his hands.

A figure appeared to form out of the light. The light vanished.

Rexus drew his battle axe from behind his back.

"Wait!" Lucifer hissed. "It is one of our brothers."

"It is Mikmash, my Lord," Rexus stuttered, gaping at Mikmash. "The last we heard—he had failed to send in his report."

A confused-looking Mikmash prostrated himself before the throne.

Lucifer adjusted himself on his seat and peered at Mikmash. "I believe we have seen the work of God in this appearance. Please, my brother, explain how you got here."

Mikmash rose then described every detail of his capture, his conversations with the humans, his suspected weakness of the human mind, and his last seconds before he vanished.

"It was the plant," said Mikmash. "I'm sure of it. This reed must have some type of power over us. Maybe it's the work of God? Maybe it's just happenstance?"

"Describe this reed?" asked Lucifer.

"I am not sure I can adequately describe it. My touch was brief. The plant did look out of place as if perhaps it belonged elsewhere than on earth."

"So it happens we do have a weak link in our armor after all," Lucifer said. "These humans must never learn this!" Lucifer clenched his fists. "Brother Mikmash, return to the surface at once and locate this plant. Show it to us. Once we know what it looks like we can avoid it. Eventually, we will exterminate this abomination if possible." He waved at Mikmash dismissively. "Now go!"

Mikmash lowered his head. "My Lord." He spoke with reverence then turned and exited. Immediately he headed for the surface.

The proverbial achilles heel was discovered. A simple touch of a plant could send a Reprobi back to hell in mere seconds. Was this a plant on earth by chance or perhaps it was designed by God who had always known this day would come? Regardless of the answer, it was a threat to the rise of the Reprobi.

CHAPTER 24

THE ENEMY OF MY ENEMY IS MY FRIEND

No building on the American continent could truly be called old, but the church meeting house standing for over seventy-five years was well on its way. It was built on a strong stone foundation held up by solid red brick below a tall, ivory white steeple with a simple gold cross that stretched to the sky. This house of God was selected for the American army to meet in and discuss an alliance with the British. A perfect location considering an evil squall was blowing towards them both.

An entire regiment of Continental infantry with two cannons surrounded the church. On the dirt path that led to its entrance, Washington stood with his chosen cadre waiting for the arrival of the British delegation. Major-General Marquis de Lafayette, Colonel Alexander Hamilton, Brigadier-General Benedict Arnold, and Chief Shenandoah were selected for the meeting. The American officers each brought a junior officer to assist them. Shenandoah brought with him Agwalongdong also known as Good Peter.

Washington kicked his boot heel, sending a small plume of smoke dust into the air.

"George, do not fret," Arnold said. "They will agree to join us." His bow lips smiled emphasizing plump cheeks and a Romanesque nose. Combined with his large brown eyes he always reminded Washington of a chipmunk.

Washington returned a deadpan look at Arnold. "I say, truly the alliance is a sure thing, yet whom shall marshal't the combined forces? We know the land the best, surely they might not but see that?"

The sight of approaching horsemen in bright red uniforms caught the men's attention. The British cavalry force moved to reveal an enclosed two horse-drawn carriage that broke from the center of their formation. The carriage approached with the sound of dirt and stone kicked up as it moved up the gravel dirt path. Along with large ornate wooden wheels, this carriage built for comfort was painted ivory white with decorative gold trim. It was driven by two well-dressed coachmen in black with silver livery. The carriage came to a halt. General Henry Clinton, commander of the British campaign, came out with four aides-de-camp.

Clinton approached Washington then gave a short nod. "General Washington"

Washington gave an equally short nod. "General Clinton," Washington said.

Washington motioned. "May I introduce to you Chief John Shenandoah, leader of the combined forces of the Five Nation Haudenosaunee Confederacy, comprising the Mohawk, Onondaga, Oneida, Cayuga, and Seneca."

"I am honored," Clinton said. He shook Shenandoah's hand.

Washington pointed to the church. "Shall we, gentlemen? There is much to discuss."

They followed inside the church. Their shoes stepped on soft dirt. The hardwood floor was missing. They moved to the center of the room.

"Sorry, no seats," Washington said. "I had to borrow the table. The furnishings were used for firewood. It appears Lieutenant Colonel Samuel Birch of the 17th Dragoons did a great job gutting the building for horse practice."

Clinton's face turned a brief flash of red. "Indeed," he said, "I regret that hath been performed. That's beyond us now." A soft cough. "Let us get down to business. General Washington, I have given your correspondence serious thought. I understand you know the land better than us, yet we bring the larger of the forces to bear. We will hast command!"

Washington's eyes grew large. "We must hast command. This is our land. This is . . ."

Chief Shenandoah whistled loudly. All eyes turned to him.

"We cannot possibly hope to win if we do not join completely now," Shenandoah said. "This is evil we go against. The grizzled warrior's face stopped briefly at each man. His wrinkled face caused by worries past and worries present looked upon them as if they were misbehaving children.

"Perhaps a simple decision tool is needed." He pulled out a coin from his pants pocket. "May I suggest we leave it to divine fate? Let us flip a coin?"

"Agreed," Washington said with a frown.

"Agreed," Clinton said with a frown.

"Good. If both sides are unhappy then it is a fair deal," Shenandoah said. "The colonial army will have heads and the British will have the opposite side." Shenandoah tossed the coin. It spun in the air, then with a clank, it struck the dirt. "Heads!"

General Clinton stood up proudly. "So, fate will have it. Washington, I am your second. What are your orders?"

Washington's face relaxed. "Come with me," he said.

Washington and Clinton walked side by side followed by their aids. They entered a small room at the back of the church. This room retained its wooden floor. A table filled with rolled maps stood at the end of the room.

Washington unrolled a large map of the northern colonies. The map depicted terrain features including mountains and river locations.

"You see here." Washington pointed to the map. "Would we get 'em into this valley, surrounded by these mountains, there is a gap that opens into it. We plug it with heavy cannons and the majority of forces. Then we push towards 'em, smashing 'em to pieces with an artillery bombardment." He cast a frown and gave a soft sigh. "To pull this off, we'll need bait. We hast a good imagining where this evil is based on areas the scouts are not returning back from. We send a force large enough to provoke 'em, and then they fall back hither." He poked his finger hard on the map. "It could be a suicide mission. Wherein the evil pursues this force, they may be caught then pounded to oblivion."

Benedict Arnold cleared his throat theatrically. He stood up straight. "It is a peril that is necessary. I would be deeply honored to lead this mission."

Every eye in attendance looked at Arnold. A few faces looked to argue for their own appointment, unintelligible mutters were heard until Washington silenced them by patting Arnold on the shoulder. He smiled. "It is yours, General. I hast confidence in you."

Arnold beamed with praise. His eyes sparkled.

Clinton scratched his head. "This seems like a sound strategy. With all our combined artillery to bear, it should'st be enough to take the field from them."

"Then we are agreed on this course," Washington said. "Let's make haste. If they gain a foothold, it may be more difficult to stop them. Yet ere we set to work gentlemen, let us toast our alliance."

Billy entered with a large tray filled with glasses of rum. The assembly waited till everyone present held a glass full.

"Put thy trust in God, men, and keep thy powder dry," Washington pronounced.

"Hear, hear," echoed in the room. Together they drank the liquor with one gulp.

With the toast completed, Washington went over his battle plans in detail.

"And that gentleman is the plan," Washington said.

He shot a few glances at the gathered men. They seemed troubled. As well as they should with the danger the Reprobi represented. He stepped towards Peter. "I have heard you are an excellent pastor. May you send us out with a prayer of protection."

"Dear God, please be with the men and women who bravely serve their communities," Peter said. "I ask you to give 'em your protection, that you be their guiding force at the head of their army, and their rearguard who keeps 'em safe from behind. We ask that you would draw 'em to yourself amidst the dangers they will face, for you are the truth, the way, and the light. Amen."

With spirits lifted with prayer, the meeting was adjourned. Washington escorted Clinton and his entourage back to their carriage.

Clinton was the last to step into the carriage. Before he entered, he turned to Washington. "I see the wisdom in your eyes. The Lord has ordained us well. I will see preparations are made in haste."

Washington held out his hand. "I know that you will see everything is out of its shell, my lobster back friend."

Clinton cocked his eyes then he shook Washington's hand in a firm grip. He gave him a wink. "I know you will Yankee doodle, who stuck a feather in a cap to call it macaroni."

After the carriage rolled off, Washington stood a few minutes in thought. Washington looked up at the sky. A strong breeze moved in the heavily clouded sky, causing the light of the sun to ebb and flow.

Dear Lord, he prayed silently. *I do not understand the abomination we fight but I know it's not of this world. It is evil. I beseech you to aid us. Grant us what is needed to destroy this abomination.*

A vision entered the mind of Washington. The light was glorious and seemed to sparkle. He squinted his eyes, fighting the brilliance. His mind was at peace in a perfect nirvana of relaxation. He wiggled his fingers and felt warm water. He lay floating on his back, pulled by a gentle current down the river. The current pulled him to a pebble beach shore. He stood up, oblivious to his clothes dripping wet. He took in deep breaths of fresh air as he made his way off the beach. He reached out and touched the reeds. In a flash, his vision ended. The vision he remembered. He knew there was meaning but he could not decipher its mystery.

CHAPTER 25

A SECOND CHANCE

Late morning sunshine breathed on the combined strength of the British, American, and Native allies. The smell of woodland just after the rain, mixed in with the distinctive smell of meat cooking, floated through their encampment. A narrow path twisted around crowded tents filled with a sea of uniformed men of all colors, the most prominent was British red, Militia white, and Continental blue.

The bivouac tents were as mismatched as the combined force. Native and Colonial American soldiers were housed in canopies imported to the colonies from a number of countries, made from linen and hempen threads in every size, shape, and color imaginable. The British with their supplies unhindered had uniformly white, linen wall tents. With volunteers arriving daily, not enough tents were available and crude brush huts were constructed wherever there was room.

Nathaniel sat alone on a damp, wooden stump listening to his iron teapot boil water. He removed the pot off the hot coals then poured scalding water down the barrel of his musket gingerly, then taking a dirty rag he capped the end of the barrel. He shook vigorously, trying not to let any water escape. After a few shakes, he poured out black water, the sort of blackness found in unknown deep pits. He repeated the process until the barrel ran clear. Satisfied with the inside of the barrel he moved to the surface. He took an oily rag from his haversack. With a mix of cold campfire ash, spit, and elbow grease he worked the rust spots. After a final wipe down, he then sharpened his saber. He scraped the curved, single-edged blade along a wet stone, working the blade. He accidentally nicked his thumb on the blade then sucked his finger. With a satisfied look, he sheathed the blade.

Lieutenant Ethan Davis and Sergeant Abner Smith approached. Their faces said they were exhausted but their eyes held a spark of resolve.

"Aaah, I could use some tea," Abner said, letting out a loud yawn. "Up all night till dark drellin den making sure they are not up to any shenanigans."

"Well, then go brew some," Nathaniel balked. He pulled a bag of tea leaves from his pocket then tossed it to Abner.

"I will take that offer," Abner said with a grin. "It's mighty fine o' de Bretts to give oehs sahme tea even after we threw a shipload o' it into the bahston harbor not dat lahng ago."

Ethan and Abner rolled over nearby stumps then took a seat.

Abner pinched tea leaves into a dented tin cup then poured the remaining water from Nathaniel's teapot. He blew on the contents then took a sip. "Aah, dat's de spaht."

A middle-aged, African-American dressed in Militia attire approached the campfire. His cheekbones were high and prominent, showing a handsome face. His nose, brown eyes, and dark black hair gave him an air of an African prince in disguise.

He poured out small spoonfuls of fire cake batter from a large cast-iron pot, just enough batter for one cake per man, on stones closest to the fire. The mix showed finely-chopped potatoes added in. Another gift from the British.

Ethan rose from his seat. "Captain, I have the pleasure of introducing you to Cato Bannister. We received him today from the 1st Rhode

Island Regiment to help fill the numbers in our company. I know Cato from back home; he's an ardent patriot." He tsked with a shake of his head. "An early enlistee in the fight for Liberty, although he has yet to have his own. He left an apprenticeship to a Mr. Elkana Humphrey of Barrington, Rhode Island, who will receive interest paid to him for his use." Ethan glanced at Cato slyly. "A little over 100 pounds. Isn't that right, Cato?"

Cato gave a hint of a frown then nodded yes.

Nathaniel stood up then shook Cato's hand. "I'm glad to see ye here in the cause for Liberty, Cato. May the Lord bless and protect you. Please be seated. What remains in the pan looks like just enough for one meal."

Cato scooped the remaining mix onto a hot stone. He cast eyes for a place to sit.

Nathaniel moved aside and motioned to the stump he was using. "Please."

Cato sat. When the mixture bubbled, he turned the cake with a nearby stick.

Abner grinned, as he touched the fringes on Cato's coat. "Ye have soehch a pretty unifahrm, though I can't ordain it do be more cahmfortable dan dis." He placed a finger through a hole through his well-worn, navy-blue Continental coat.

The Militia uniform—in contrast to the Continental uniform—was similar to how Native Americans dressed. They wore a white hunting shirt, ornamented with a great many fringes, somewhat resembling a wagoner's frock. Tied around the waist was a broad belt, to which was fastened a tomahawk, a shot bag, and a carved powder horn.

"Ethan says you enlisted early. Tell me why, Cato?" Nathaniel said.

Cato's eyes lit up. "Never thought I'd see myself going against the British Army. I serve of my own accord to compose 'em to pay for the burning of Falmouth. The bastards' navy bombarded Falmouth from morning 'till evening. After the bombardment ended, they dispatched a landing party into town and set fire to the buildings they hadn't destroyed. To attack innocent civilians. It just ain't right." He hesitated. "Not right at all, I say!"

Abner harrumphed, "I'll tell you one thing, I segned up to kell red coats, naht dese Reprobi things."

"I'll kill anything to protect my family and home," Cato said. He grabbed the hot cake off the stone then tossed it from one hand to another. He blew on it then took a bite.

"Although we don't fight the British, we are still fighting for liberty," Nathaniel said. "And your liberty is secured now that Washington will free every slave that serves with us."

"Hear, hear," said Ethan. "I ne'r fear the British. These creatures, I do. It will not be easy." He stretched out his legs. "Tell you one thing, I can't wait to get home, to get up in the morning without worrying about if today will be my last."

"If we finish these ungodly hordes, then make peace with the British, we can be home soon," Nathaniel said. "A hard beginning does make a good ending."

Ethan tossed a small stick into the fire pit, and the glowing orange embers lit it. The flames burned hungrily. "It feels like forever since I've been home. I miss my old dog. We named him Tray. So faithful and gentle. There will ne'r be another like him. I also miss the old songs sung at my local tavern. I'm losing memory of how they go."

"Lieutenant, I have ne'r seen you so glum," Nathaniel said. "Your presence normally grants energy to us all. Although I figured soldiering would eventually catch up with you. Take heart, we are looking good. I believe never a combined force has been arrayed so committed to its goal. Not since the ancient Persians launched the invasion of Greece, anyhow."

Abner scratched his chin. "Do ye remember de Battle of Thermopylae between King Leonidas of Sparta and de three hundred holding de pass against the Persians? Do noehmbers really cooehnt? Methinks 'tis smartness dat wens a battle."

A red-uniformed British soldier bumped into Nathaniel. To anyone watching it would have appeared the soldier was simply not paying attention. The hit was hard enough for Nathaniel to lose balance and nearly fall. The soldier did not stop. He continued walking as if the blow did not happen.

"'Ey there!" Abner growled. The soldier froze.

Nathaniel recognized there was no rank insignia indicating the soldier's rank as private. Excuse me, soldier," he said. "We agreed to respect rank here! But regardless of rank we do not blindly knock into someone then show them no courtesy!"

The private's shoulders slumped visibly then he whirled his head looking away as if he would bolt.

Nathaniel took a closer look at the man's face. *Why does he look so nervous? It's as if he is hiding something.* He spotted something in the soldier's eyes. He could swear they looked a shade redder than eyes should actually be.

"What regiment do you belong to?" Nathaniel said. His hand slipped to the handle of his pistol held by the waistband of his belt.

The soldier looked dumbstruck. "I belong to the third regiment," he sputtered, then turned his back.

"Oh really?" Nathaniel grabbed the man's shoulder firmly. "Who is your commander? I would like a word with him."

The soldier turned around. "A captain," he said with serious spittle coming from his mouth.

"Captain *who?*" Abner said as he took a step towards the soldier.

The man's face contorted in anguish, then quickly into a rage. In a spin, he pulled his bayonet attached to his belt then lunged at Nathaniel with it. Nathaniel caught the man's elbow, but with forward momentum, they both fell towards the fire pit. Nathaniel rolled away at the last moment. The soldier fell face-forward into the hot orange coals. He did not holler or cry as his flesh burned to make an ungodly smell.

The men tread backward as they watched the burned soldier stand up, flesh melted, one eye shut, but leaving one eye unmarred. The iris of the remaining eye looked at Nathaniel with unbridled hatred. Nathaniel pulled his pistol out, aimed then cocked it.

In a rush, the soldier charged. A shot rang out. The possessed man took a hit to his mouth. Teeth bits exploded from his mouth. Ethan intercepted him, punching him on the left side of his head at the same time as Abner crashed his fist into the right side of his head. The soldier bent over. Nathaniel kicked him in the head. The man slumped to the ground.

"Tie him up," Nathaniel said. "Praise God, it looks like we have another Reprobi captive."

Drums beat as the Allied infantry departed their encampment in long columns. Calvary followed with the thud of hooves and the creak of saddle leather. At the side of the long column, field cannons were pulled by large wheeled carriages, surrounded by their trained gun crews on horseback. These "galloper guns" would be the lynchpin of the offensive, the means to plug the gap and devastate the Reprobi army. With the Reprobi in the correct location, the carriages would race up, unlimbering their cannon then deliver a devastating volley. If the gun crews failed to complete their burden, the Reprobi could escape and the allied army wiped out.

The bait force led by General Benedict Arnold left a day early to find and stir up the Reprobi nest. They knew the best place to start searching. The location where scouts disappeared and never returned.

Breathing in the fresh woodland air, Nathaniel stood, watching the army pass. His emotions were controlled, unlike his rapid heartbeat. He wished he could be in the thick of the fighting, but he had his orders. His entire company was entrusted again to guard and learn from their captive. His mind ran through every detail from his previous encounter with the Reprobi named Mikmash.

Nathaniel made his way to the prisoner absorbed in thought. *This time I will actually get something useful from the prisoner. So help me God!*

The Reprobi, possessed in a man's body, sat cross-legged in his cell next to a human corpse. Flies had already started to buzz around the bloated body. The body was dressed in a grey frock coat, a cream-colored vest with matching breeches, with white lace orna-mental frill on the front of his shirt and cuffs. Baron von Steuben had entered the cell alone to try and get answers but he failed. The conversation was going well when the Reprobi reached out and broke the Baron's neck with a snap. Nobody dared to open the cell yet to remove the corpse.

Approaching the cell Nathaniel fought back the panic and urge to vomit.

"Your true name, if you hast one?" Nathaniel asked.

"The name my brothers call me is Lucivia."

"I do crave to know something? How do you possess and take over this body?"

"Quite easily, in fact, we can do this at any time, Son of Adam," Lucivia said. "Let me go or I'll command your body next." He contorted in a grimace. "This I promise you!" He spit.

"Methinks not; you would hast escaped already," replied Nathaniel. "Whither is your true form hiding? Allow us to know. We will collect it and return it to you. You are captured. Why possess this man's body anymore? What use is it to you?"

Lucivia produced a sinister laugh. "I don't think ssso. I kinda like this body. Although it lacks somewhat in durability. Oh, this man will get his body back at some point, but not 'till I mutilate him so he can remember me. If you set me free, I can re-enter my body and release him back to you."

Nathaniel shook his head. "I will ask you another question. A good answer and you may be rewarded. Tell me about this?"

Nathaniel held up a green reed from a horsetail plant. Lucivia could not help but wince.

"By the look on your face, I see 'tis important. There seems to be a lot of talk about horsetail. I don't know a single horse with its full tail, yet sadly a horse's tail appears to be useless against you. Tracks led to an escaped Reprobi in a patch of this plant. All traces of our guest Mikmash disappeared. We do lack answers, and you desire to be free.

Grant me the answers I want and I warrant to set you free." Nathaniel jingled the keys to the cell.

Lucivia stared blankly at the ground; he visualized what could happen to his brothers if he gave out the information. However, freedom beckoned as it does to all living things. The desire for freedom was too much a cross to bear. *They will find out anyway, at some point.* He thought to justify his thinking.

"If we touch the plant you hold, it sends us back to hell," he said. "Now set me free as you promised!"

Nathaniel looked at Lucivia incredulously. "Methinks not. You are not the only one of God's creatures that can lie. Gramercy for your information. It shall be most valuable, I'm sure."

Nathaniel turned then walked away.

Lucivia threw himself at the cage bars. He slammed his body over and over again, determined to smash his way out. In human form, he didn't stand a chance. The result of his efforts was broken rib bones and a bruised ego.

CHAPTER 26

DELIVERED FROM HELL

Deep below the earth's crust, Lucifer stood alone barefoot in his throne chamber. One solitary candle remained to flicker on the stone wall. His other candles were allowed to burn out. In near darkness, he crossed his arms to look at his throne. The throne was like an unwanted lover he was glad to leave. *Soon!* his mind screamed. *I depart from hell to lead my brothers. The pages will turn quickly now, but I still hold a question. Why has God still not spoken to me?* Instinctively, he nearly prayed to God for guidance. Although he had been banished to his prison, he had been in heaven far longer. His apprehension shrunk with Rexus entering the chamber. Answers or not, freedom, an almost forgotten dream, was about to begin.

Rexus prostrated himself then rose.

"My Lord, we are ready," he said.

Lucifer nodded. His red eyes gave his throne an icy stare. "Did you bring what I asked for, my brother?" he asked.

"Yes, my Lord." Rexus handed Lucifer a large iron sledgehammer massive enough that two hands would be needed to swing it. Lucifer swung the hammer, knocking off one of the stone arms. Stone fragments flew everywhere with every hammer strike as he pulverized the remainder of the throne. "My old friend, I will not be coming back," he hissed softly.

After the throne was demolished to rubble, Lucifer dressed for his ascension. He slipped on his heavy-soled, hobnailed sandals, called *caligae*. His armor was next, the *lorica segmentata* that consisted of metal iron strips fastened to internal leather straps with shoulder guards. Breastplates and backplates added further protection. He placed on his head a thin metal, Spartan-looking helmet with cutouts for his horns. Out of a crevice of a rock, he pulled out a golden scepter with an image of a serpent swallowing a bird of prey, talons still showing, at the top of it. He tied it to his waist. He thumbed it in thought. *If you want to rule over mankind, you will have to play the part of an emperor.*

He gave a final glance at the pile of rubble then walked out of his chamber with his head held high.

Rexus walked by his side to the gateway to hell. A simple wooden ladder led through a tunnel to the surface. Lucifer climbed up the ladder.

Horns sounded as Lucifer stepped onto the earth. The sunlight blinded him temporarily, causing him to squint. With deep breaths, he waited for his eyes to adjust. He could smell the long-forgotten scent of forest air. His eyes adjusted to see the entire Reprobi army of 6,666 strong. They stood in perfect battle formation, shields up, shoulder to shoulder. Atticus stepped forward carrying the red flag standard. It blew gently in the breeze.

Lucifer knelt on one knee, reached out his hand, and grabbed a clump of earth. He watched as the tiny particles rolled off his fingers and through his hands.

"*Terra*, for now, my brothers!" Lucifer cried. "The future shall return us to heaven in glory!"

"My Lord!" the Reprobi resounded as one.

A carved wooden chair made to resemble a throne carried by long poles was brought and lowered to the ground. He mounted the chair then it was raised. A large two-handed scythe was handed to him. He tightly clenched the long handle. With one arm, he raised the scythe.

"My friends, we rebelled against God and were forsaken. The Father was unfair to imprison us. The tears of myself and my brethren have carved rivers below the earth. I wanted only freedom for you. He would make us slaves. It was my love for you that released us. The Father, Son, and Holy Spirit are absent." *Where are you now?* I wonder. "We have his favor to rule over the Sons of Adam. They have displeased him for the last time. We will deliver justice to them. They will serve us as it was meant to be."

Lucifer raised his scythe. A bright white sheep was brought over beside him. The creature bleated in fright. With a lunge, he slashed the lamb with a swipe powerful enough to sever the lamb in half. With blood running off his blade, he spoke:

"It is only a short walk to our destiny. Follow me, my brothers, and I will give you eternity, eternity to do what you choose. Forward, my brethren, to liberty and freedom!"

With feverish hissing cries, the Reprobi slapped their blades to their shields. The combined sound crescendoed to a furious pitch. The sound unleashed onto the forest cut deep, frightening earthy creatures that listened. Birds broke for the air, deer bounded off, and every living creature that heard fled. The greatest threat the earth had ever known had just been released.

CHAPTER 27
FRESH BAIT

A s if the heat of the moment was not enough, the weather had turned stifling. For days, the temperature stood well above 90 degrees. Regardless of the summer blaze, the bait mission would commence. The participants would bear their sweat like a christening before a battle.

Benedict Arnold lowered his telescope, a gift from Washington. The telescope featured a brass section that slid into a wood section. He knew the Reprobi encampment lay before him somewhere, the latest scouts sent in had not returned. It was well known that the planned attack on them would be memorialized as a dangerous operation, like the famous Battle of Melanthius, which took place in 559, between foreign invaders against the Byzantine Empire. Under the skilled command of General Belisarius, who was brought out of retirement, a force of only three hundred veterans and conscripts defeated an invasion by much greater numbers. Their elite force may not survive but even if they failed, Arnold would be remembered through time as a hero, statues would be erected in his honor, and this pleased his ego.

The attack force was made up of four hundred men, splintered into mobile units of fifty. The best marksmen and scouts from the British, Colonials, and Native Americans waited to advance. Washington prayed the force was large enough to provoke the Reprobi to pursue them. They waited until dusk to begin the attack. It was reasoned that this was best to hide their numbers and they might catch the Reprobi by surprise.

Thomas Shenandoah, Arnold's second-in-command, crouched down next to him, bow out in front. Thomas held an air of confidence that Arnold secretly coveted. Arnold would have liked to pick his subordinate, but Washington was insistent on Thomas. The Native troops were by far the best scouts the Allies had available. Thomas had done a remarkable job of positioning the men. As far as they knew the Reprobi had not spotted them.

With sweat trickling down their backs Arnold and Thomas patiently waited for the wood smell that would signal the Reprobi were settling in for the night.

Arnold whispered to Thomas, "The men are in place. I'm thinking the Reprobi haven't seen us. It's close enough to darkness. We should'st begin the attack now while we hast the element of surprise."

Thomas locked eyes with Arnold. "We want to keep to the resolve we agreed on. Their campfires shall say to us when 'tis dark enough. It is best to hide our numbers. The darkness shall grant us cover while we go into attack positions. They must regard they are going after the entire Army. Should they not send the entire force to pursue us, we fail. The lives of many rests with us. There is only one thing harder than looking for a dewdrop in the dew or fishing for a quahog without a rake, and that is patience. I feel your restlessness. Please, stick to the plan."

Arnold's face reddened. "I am in command here!" he snapped. "The decision lies with me alone. Sometimes a commander must seize the instant."

Thomas let out a soft sigh. "I recognize that, but Washington's orders supersede yours," Thomas said. "Too much is counting on us."

Han appeared. His appearance looked menacing with his painted war face and build.

Arnold gulped, "Agreed."

Han spoke, "I have just returned. Those Reprobi are certainly arrogant. A dozen of them are literally asleep at their posts. They must think us incapable of attack."

Arnold licked his lips. "Good, just a little longer now."

Han cocked his head. Han raised an eyebrow. "Someone approaches. He may as well be crashing through the forest."

General Peter Muhlenberg came out of the brush then knelt down beside them. General Muhlenberg was placed as third in command. He cared very little about the command order as long as it offered a chance to fight Reprobi.

"Gentlemen," Muhlenberg said, "a final prayer before battle. Please bow your heads." They dipped their heads. "Deliver us from our adversaries, O Lord, for they are false witnesses that rise against us, and such as speak wrong. They do not belong to the earth of the living. We ask you to guide the aim of our rifles, to stir up our strength to do your bidding. The eyes of the Lord are righteous. The righteous cry, we know the Lord heareth them and will deliver them out of their troubles so that we may better glorify thee. Amen."

As the last words were spoken the distinct scent of burning wood trickled into the nose of Thomas. It was time. He gave an air-rending owl call.

The force moved quickly into their final positions. They made sounds, but the expert scouts made far less than a typical soldier clamoring through the woods. They found stones to step on, fallen logs to leap on or run nimbly along them.

While on his knees, Thomas pulled the string back on his bow then fired an arrow into a tree one hundred feet away. A few seconds later, long distant flights of arrows flew into the Reprobi camp. Arrows struck the Reprobi guards, but they batted most of them off like toothpicks. However, they served their purpose to give them pause. Concentrated musket fire then erupted into them. This dropped a few but not as many as they hoped. Reprobi raised their tall rectangular shields, making a firm defense.

Then, it rained mobile artillery. Mortars and small cannons that were small enough to be carried burst into them. This time, the Reprobi were rattled; they swarmed around like a hornet's nest just kicked. Many Reprobi fell, unable to get up. Quickly, more Reprobi came out of whatever hole they hid in. They began to form into ranks. Well . . . some did, but some charged headlong to engage the attackers. Many took multiple hits, some with arms blown off but they still kept coming. The split units, with the exception of the artillery, converged rapidly and focused fire. Arnold, Thomas, and Muhlenberg commanded from the center.

As the sky continued to darken the battle quickly descended into chaos. Under torchlight, the attacking force kept firing volleys until a Reprobi charge left them engaged in hand-to-hand combat. The Reprobi viciously attacked—a rush of blades, fangs, and eyes looking for blood. Men fought, cried out, moaned, and died. The sound of artillery grew silent, their position was located and they were slaughtered to the last man.

Thomas dodged a gladius aimed at his belly. Fortunately, Muhlenberg came in with a bayonet strike piercing the creature's head. The bayonet went through its eye, and with enough force, came out the other side of its head. Arnold shot his pistol at the Reprobi's other eye. The Reprobi took a knee as Muhlenberg came from behind and severed off its head with a blow from his saber.

"It is the time!" Thomas hollered. "We have their attention. We've done what we can. We must hope they will pursue us!"

"Agreed! Before we all perish!" Arnold said as he reloaded his pistol.

At the top of his lungs, Thomas cried out, "Oonah, oonah!" Warriors in earshot returned the call in unison. "Oonah, oonah!" Thomas knew there should have been more voices that returned the call. But many bodies lay scattered among the earth they fought and died for.

A bugle horn echoed through the night air calling for retreat. They ran like hell. The mission was a success; the entire Reprobi army chased after them with vengeance on their brains towards the gap. There was a chance the remainder of Arnold's force could survive; if they could make it to the horses, set aside for them. The horses would increase their mobility and chances of escape.

Arnold, Muhlenberg, and Thomas ran alongside each other with half the initial force surrounding them.

"Praise be to God, we're alive after all!" Arnold said as he breathed heavily. "We fought magnificently! Truly a glorious battle to be remembered!"

Thomas shrugged as he ran. "There is nothing glorious about men dying in battle. A peaceful death with old age is better for them."

Arnold missed an exposed root and face-planted, knocking the wind out of him. Thomas and Muhlenberg each grabbed one of Arnold's arms and half-dragged him along while he caught his breath. They heard the neigh of horses.

A sharp pain crossed Thomas's back. He turned, dropping the arm of Arnold. A Reprobi with heat in his eyes lashed out again with his axe. Muhlenberg turned and kicked the Reprobi in the stomach. The Reprobi stood solid, ignoring the kick. He gave a twisted grin. With a gigantic swing, the Reprobi took Muhlenberg's head off. The head dropped then rolled several times, the body fell with the neck squirting blood. Arnold fired a pistol shot point-blank at the Reprobi's face and it stumbled back, missing its nose.

"Let's go; the pastor,s with God now!" Arnold blurted out. He bounded away without looking back.

A stunned Thomas ran after Arnold a trail of blood dripping from his shirt. He became dizzy, his steps faltered. A strong hand grabbed his unwounded shoulder. Han's blood-bathed face met his. "I have you, brother."

The survivors made it to the horses. Their numbers reduced again, nearly a hundred remained. Untying the horses from the trees they mounted them quickly then galloped off. Horses flew scattered through the woods followed by swift-moving Reprobi. The horses were not as fast as they thought. The Reprobi in long strides were able to catch some. They hunted then butchered their prey. By the time the Allied force approached the gap only fifty remained.

CHAPTER 28

VICTORY OR DEATH

Tuckered and mosquito-bitten, the Allied Army trudged onward. Quick-passing thunderstorms poured rain, turning the dusty roads into sludge. The mud and annoying bites were cumbersome but nothing was going to prevent Washington from his intended destination. When the rain stopped, rapidly thinning gray clouds let through startlingly bright sunshine with vivid blue sky. A beautiful double rainbow formed, stretching across the sky, its colorful hues kissed the earth. However, there would be no pot of gold at the end of it, no treasure. The end of the rainbow was the direction the Reprobi would be coming, that is, if the bait force was successful.

Reaching their destination, the Army deployed into position. The combined Colonial, British, and Native army numbered 28,000 men, including 3,000 colonials recruited from the countryside, many good hunters that could easily hit a moving target.

Their first task was to set up the cannons, the key to the battle plan. Every cannon available was placed in position. The British General, Henry Clinton, would personally command the artillery in the upcoming battle.

The battle plan was straightforward: Arnold's bait force would lead the Reprobi into the gap. Once the gap was plugged via concentrated artillery fire the Reprobi would move into a valley a mile long and wide that ended at a large mountain. The hills on the sides of the valley held large siege and fort cannons drawn up there by teams of horses. A massive barrage of cannons would unleash hellfire from above. The infantry would then be sent in to clean up the scraps. The plan did rely on a little bit of luck. The Reprobi first needed to fall for the bait. Washington had sufficient numbers and confidence to land a knockout blow. He knew that no battle ever went according to plan, even the best. It is said greatness is finding victory after plans begin to fall apart. Washington did not know what he would do if the plan failed. There was no backup plan or plan B. If they failed, he believed they would all be slaughtered. Their corpses likely used in a grotesque monument to their failure. Washington was determined to lead the forces to victory or die on the battlefield.

If Hamilton could not have breakfast this morning, at least a strong tea would do. With a yawn, he tossed a few thin sticks of kindling into dying embers. He blew on them till they burst into flames. He grabbed from his pack a small copper tea kettle, filled it with water then placed it on orange coals just outside the flames.

First Lafayette appeared then other officers to sit on the ground around the fire. The water was steaming in the kettle when Hamilton took it off the coals. He placed a tiny cloth sack filled with tea leaves and let it sit in it for a few minutes, then he poured a cup for himself. The remainder of the pot was handed to Lafayette, who poured a cup for himself.

Hamilton and Lafayette sat back-to-back drinking the tea. The tea did help remove some of the fog from lack of good sleep. The imported East India Company tea was good Congou black tea. It brewed a deep transparent red liquid with a strong yet pleasant bitter flavor. The addition of milk would surely add to the enjoyment of the beverage if it was present.

Hamilton frowned. "Would I lived a thousand years, I do not think I would understand what is happening hither yet I do know that history shall judge what happens here."

"May these words grant you some peace, my friend," Lafayette said. "Chief Shenandoah told me some wise words. Our destiny is planned from the beginning. We are yet only participants in its design. There is no need to worry if the issue is already known. Never try to swim against the current; it is a useless exercise."

Hamilton released a soft sigh. "Wise words indeed. I do draw comfort from them." He took another sip of tea.

"I do wish the French army was here with us," Lafayette said. "They are probably already on their way. Alas, they shall ne'r compose it in time."

"Say to me, are you homesick for your country?"

"I have found brothers hither to embrace. We have formed friendships in days of peril and glory. I am not homesick. Someday I shall return to mine country, for now, this is mine country."

"You shall always be welcome hither, and perhaps one-day mine country will return the favor to France, to be there in the hour of your nation's want. Maybe they shall cry out 'Lafayette, we are here!'"

They scrambled to their feet as Washington approached them.

"At ease, gentlemen," Washington said. Bags under his eyes gave his face the appearance his body was weary but his eyes cast alertness.

"Please remain sitting." The men sat back down. "I wish to thank all of you for your service. None of you hast signed up for this. I see many youthful faces hither. Our youth we can have today. In heaven hides our book of fate. May we have the blessings to grow old for our sake. Be it known that if you perish unwitting of the coming battle, if you fall and your soul is sent to the pearly gates, know that you will never see darkness again. Death is only a door that leads to the light."

Lafayette looked up. "We understand what we fight for and what would befall us would we lose. We are content to grant our lives to win this victory."

Hamilton looked up. "You are like the great Caesar," Hamilton added. "We are confident you will lead us to victory." He raised his voice for the entire group to hear. "Huzzah! Victory to mankind!"

As one, the group of officers shouted "Huzzah! Huzzah!"

Washington used his hands to signal them to lower their voices. "I applaud your spirits. 'Tis essential to maintain positive morale. Do your best to keep the men under your command positive. It shall not be long now ere the shadow of death arrives."

Late afternoon, distant gunfire was heard. A few shots at first, then a peppering sound signaling a large engagement. The role of drums called the army immediately to form. The massive army arrayed in long rows to either side of Washington who stood at the center surrounded by his Guard. In front of the infantry, the artillerymen prepared the cannon to fire.

The line broke to let in a rider who immediately reported to Washington.

Although the rider clutched his arm and blood dripped from his blood-soaked shirt, he held a look of confidence.

"General, dispatch from Arnold," the rider said. "He doth wish to let you know the Reprobi are following close behind. They are driven by a need to continue moving forward."

Washington did not have to wait long to see the proof. Horses flew by, followed by a glimpse of colorful Reprobi in pursuit. If he could have seen their eyes up close, he would have seen pure hatred burned in them. For now, the Reprobi seemed oblivious to the main army in pursuit of their prey.

After Washington guessed a majority of Reprobi had entered the gap (he had no idea their true numbers), the cannons opened up, unleashing devastation volley after volley. Their thundering booms echoed for miles. For the Reprobi, it was a scene out of Dante's *Inferno*. Heavy cannonballs bounced off the ground, tearing Reprobi apart.

The smoke from the cannon fire impaired their operators' view as they loaded and fired as quickly as possible. After every three rounds they fired, they pushed the cannons forward 20 feet. General Clinton, with his guard surrounding him, moved through the grey cloud yelling, "Fire at will! Fire at will! Take it to 'em! It's liberty or death!" The grey smoke cloud grew thick, completely covering the view of the artillery from the infantry. They heard the cannon fire begin to slow even though they held plenty of ammunition. Shots and screams were heard from within the smoke.

A small force numbering one hundred Reprobi staggered out of the smoke. Each let loose their long pilla javelins. With Washington's army in tight ranks most struck a target. The barbed tips went through the soft uniforms like a knife through soft butter. The Reprobi began to form a line opposite the infantry. As the smoke cleared the Reprobi force now grew to several hundred and was continuing to grow.

Washington gave the command for the infantry to fire. Thousands of shots flew towards the Reprobi.

Hamilton grabbed a cartridge from his belt then tore it open with his mouth. After pouring the powder down the barrel, he dropped a lead ball down it then quickly rodded it. He set his musket to his shoulder. A loud crack of fire was heard, a Reprobi's serpentine face exploded in red.

"What the hell has happened to the cannons?" Lafayette said, stepping next to Hamilton.

"I don't know, but it's not good," Hamilton said. "I fear they will fight their way out of the gap. They are barely in it."

Lafayette glimpsed a man running towards them. "Hold your fire, men! Hold your fire!"

A Native scout dressed in Militia garb, with long black hair behind his back, ran toward their position; doing so uncovered his dark brown eyes set with panic.

In a frantic voice, the native spoke, "The cannons are lost! We have somehow been infiltrated! All is lost!"

Hamilton frowned. "Washington is at the center. Relay this to him. Go!"

Washington's Guard parted to let in the scout. He took the news calmly. The artillery was essential; without it, it was up to the infantry. He looked to his left and right, looking at his men then he looked up at the sky. He prayed softly in his mind. *Lord, it is such a beautiful world, help us preserve it from these creatures. This is my final appeal. We march!*

Washington drew his saber then pointed towards the Reprobi. "Advance at a walk!" Washington shouted. All along the line, officers echoed his command. Shoulder to shoulder the infantry advanced.

The Reprobi army thousands strong stood in a tight formation shield to shield as a wall of multicolored uniforms approached them. A small force broke off, numbering nearly one hundred Reprobi, charging toward the Allies in a flying wedge formation. The Reprobi's bright red standard waved at the center. They moved as quickly as a desperate cavalry charge.

Washington's officers in the front ranks watched the pointed wedge rapidly clear the distance to them. They hastily called out to their troops, shouting, "Make ready!" The call was echoed through the ranks. Then a loud bellow from Washington, "Fire!"

The front line fired then knelt down to reload as the second line discharged their muskets. The charging Reprobi were stunned by the volley of musket balls. It was a scene of carnage as the Reprobi were cut down from the heavy fire. A shield with many holes was not much protection.

A horn blew a shrill sound, the charging Reprobi stopped. They descended back into the main Reprobi force. The tight formation the Allied army saw a good distance away only moments ago, was now close to striking distance. Washington's army was so focused on the Reprobi charge that they didn't notice the brisk advance. The allies kept up the attack, firing at will, as fast as they could, praying the Reprobi did not get close enough to use their wicked blades.

Hamilton dropped to one knee, taking careful aim at what he suspected as a Reprobi officer who was pointing with his battle-axe, rallying a cluster of Reprobi. He pulled the hammer back on his rifle then squeezed the trigger. A sharp crack of fire rang out with a puff of grey smoke. The officer struck in the chest did not even blink. Without warning, there was a loud ringing sound in Hamilton's ear. Lafayette let loose a shot from his musket close to Hamilton's ear. Hamilton's ears rang as he fought through his temporary deafness. Lafayette moved forward, oblivious of his action. Hamilton froze for a few heartbeats, holding his ear.

From the corner of his eye, a vast blanket of white fog began to grow in the center of the Reprobi.

Rexus moved up and down the Reprobi ranks, his body visibly damaged. Parts of his flesh had been ripped off. An earlier hit to his mouth took out a portion of his lip and one fang. Oblivious to his wounds, he focused on the moment. Losing the battle would be far worse than any injury that was guaranteed to heal. He stood, pointing and shouting with his battle axe.

Although taller than his brothers and the only one with horns, Lucifer was unnoticed at the back of the Reprobi position; he scanned the battlefield intently. Hundreds of Reprobi littered the ground, some crawling, some unable to move. The enemy advance had collapsed on their left side. The Reprobi engaged in close combat with them. Regardless of the panic they faced, the humans held their ground. To the right of the field, the allies were having more success. With sustained musket and rifle fire, they were moving the Reprobi back. A gap opened in the center.

It is time, Lucifer thought to himself. *Time to pull the legs off these annoying gnats. Time to crush the Sons of Adam.*

Lucifer moved into the growing breach on the battlefield surrounded by Reprobi serving as body shields. He set his scythe down then he quickly dabbed a few drops of spirits on a handful of dry grey roots.

Then he struck a flint rock with his dagger. He blew on the spark. A cloud of white smoke billowed out as the roots were set ablaze. The smoke poured out, enveloping a large area. The humans paused at the sight of the white fog and refused to enter. Out of the smoke, the Reprobi century formed. In perfect unison, they raised their weapons and fired. They reloaded precisely. In disbelief, the humans looked upon them in terror.

Washington's voice could be heard. "Bear the line! For god's sake bear the line! If we fold, we are all dead! Dead!"

Washington noticed the advance on the right side began to falter. The Reprobi force filled the opening in the battlefield; in tight formation with locked shields, they advanced quickly towards the Allies. It was like a hammer hitting a nail. The Allies were butchered as they tripped over themselves to escape. Like chopped soft firewood the corpses quickly piled up.

Nathaniel glimpsed cannon ahead. *Why are they not firing?* He thought as he approached. *I hear the broil from a distance, surely they have want of 'em.* He raised his hand to signal his company to stop. The entire company, with the exception of Lieutenant Ethan leading a squad of six men, was present. Ethan scouted to the left of their position.

With a quick glimpse, he noticed bloodied corpses both humans and horses. He peeked through the brush and noticed what he thought were men guarding the cannon. No not men but two dozen Reprobi. His company outnumbered them four to one. In normal circumstances, they wouldn't stand a chance. However, Nathaniel's company brought more than numbers; they brought destruction, compliments of musket balls rubbed with horsetail. If they had time, they would have rubbed it on their bayonets but in their haste, they were unable to. Nathaniel was concerned they did not have enough ammunition prepared. Most had been prepared while on the march.

"Prepare to fire," whispered Nathaniel.

He watched a Reprobi sniff the air, then point in their direction. "Cover's blown, bahys!" cried Sergeant Abner. "Let's get dat cannahn back!"

Nathaniel hollered, "Fire!" then ran yelling, "Charge!"

With a cry of "Huzzah!" The company charged forward, Nathaniel at their lead. They made short work of the Reprobi. Anywhere horse-tail-laced musket balls hit serpentine flesh, the Reprobi faded then blinked out. No Reprobi made it at arm's length of them.

The sound of weeping was heard. Nathaniel looked down.

Molly turned over. Her face and dress were covered with blood. "'Twere awful. They infiltrated us. M-my husband, oh sweet William . . . dead!"

Fat tears rolling down her face, she pointed to a headless corpse. "I was sponging out the guns between shots when my husband's cannon was attacked!"

Nathaniel squeezed her shoulder. "It is a horrible thing that has occurred, but you can have your vengeance now. I know little about cannon. Help us let these cannons be silent no longer." He turned to his men. "Man the cannons!" he cried.

The cannons were hastily prepared. They could not man all the cannons, so they focused on the larger ones. They had the benefit of the most range. With no experienced gun crews, they were lucky a few among them had fired cannons before.

Relief flooded into Nathaniel to see Ethan approach with his men. Ethan turned to Cato. "Say to the Captain what you saw."

Cato swallowed, "Captain, I caught good glimpses of the Reprobi. They are advancing on Washington's army; it looks bleak."

"Well, let's see if we can give them a hand!" Nathaniel responded.

With tears rolling down her face, Molly fired the first cannonball.

The first volley of Iron balls overshot and ripped into Washington's collapsing lines. They knew they hit them by the screams that rang out. The cannon was elevated then fired again. This time the balls flew true to their mark. Tight lines of Reprobi were struck with devastating effects. The heavy balls hit the ground, bouncing at high speeds, kicking up earth and Reprobi limbs.

The Reprobi quickly split off a few centuries, a couple hundred, from the main force to counterattack the cannon fire. Normally it would be impossible to defend against such a quick-moving Reprobi charge but with the aid of horsetail laced balls, dozens of defenders were like a thousand. Nathaniel's company held back the attacking Reprobi while the cannon continued to pound unceasingly.

CHAPTER 29

UNTIL IT IS OVER

Atticus, his marble-colored scaly body hideously mutilated, bone and muscle exposed, still gripped the Reprobi standard. The standard riddled after hundreds of shots was shredded and tattered. In his other hand tight in his grip was his battle-axe dripping with blood.

The Legion was face to face with the enemy, in sword length, they were an effective killing machine. When the front rank reached their physical limits from fatigue or injury, they rotated out of position so that a fresh Legionnaire could take his place. The end of the gap that Washington's Army pushed them into was near.

Nathaniel's Artillery barrage began to rain from above. The Reprobi did not slow or pause as balls fell to bounce and wreaked carnage. Nothing would stop their movement with their Lord among them. The Reprobi continued to press forward.

Lucifer snarled at the sky then turned to Rexus. "The Sons of Adam have somehow taken back the cannon. Send two centuries at once to stop them!"

Rexus sent orders to his centurions then immediately returned to Lucifer's side.

With precision, two centuries split towards the back of the Legion then bolted away. Legionaries that had not seen the front yet were sent. It would not take them long for the fresh troops to reach the cannon.

Lucifer waited for the barrage to stop. Enough time passed that it was clear the attack was unsuccessful.

"Their cannons should have been silenced by now!" Lucifer hissed out loud. "How can this be?

As if in answer a ball came hurtling from the sky. It bounced then rolled, and every Reprobi it struck faded then blink out. The surrounding Reprobi paused at the site of the disappearance.

A lizardly sneer on Lucifer's lips. "They discovered horsetail! We are lost!"

"If we spread out, we can envelop them," Rexus said. "We can smash 'em still!"

A cannonball fell from behind them; it bounced up ripping off Rexus' cobra black arm.

Lucifer cackled. "Phew, in a fool's paradise. With our numbers dwindling? We will not envelope anything!" Lucifer scanned the battlefield. Thousands of men's corpses littered the battlefield with hundreds of Reprobi shredded to pieces. "So close I could taste it. But we have time. It will only be a blink of time until we defeat them. We will withdraw. The mistake was not using their technology to our advantage. We will not make that mistake again!"

Rexus picked up his torn-off arm. A look of defeat in his eyes. "Yes, my Lord."

"To me, my brothers! For a short reprise!" bellowed Lucifer as he raised his scythe.

The Legion at the front ranks kept fighting while the back ranks in precise movements fell in behind Lucifer. They picked up their fallen and wounded as they marched out, leaving no one behind for the humans. Smoke was lit to mask their escape. Their rifle unit spread out firing their remaining ammunition as the front ranks emptied to escape with their brothers. The rifle unit completely out of ammo was the last to leave the field.

Washington drew his army together then immediately called for a charge, but it was a half-hearted attempt; the men did not have the stamina to pursue their foe. The Reprobi made their escape following behind their Lord.

Alone on the battlefield, Washington walked amid the carnage. The corpses lay upon the earth. Somewhere, mothers, fathers, brothers, and sisters would learn they had died then mourn. He remained until all the dead and wounded were collected. The Army held against the Reprobi, but his heart gained little joy from this. It held mostly sorrow for those that lost their lives under his command.

The Reprobi survived. Washington failed to defeat and destroy them. The dead never complain, but he vowed to avenge their sacrifices by never giving up the fight for liberty. Against a foreign power or the Reprobi. To help build a new nation, established and represented by the citizens of an American Nation.

Washington walked off the battlefield, and beneath an old oak tree found Hamilton and Lafayette, the latter with a blood-smeared bandage around his head that covered one eye, leaning against it about to nod off from exhaustion. A gentle breeze stirred the tree. Washington closed his eyes for a moment and breathed in the air. Taking off his dusty coat, he shook it off, and then gently placed it over Hamilton and Lafayette. More work needed to be done, more blood, more sacrifice, but for now, a moment of peace. He sat down alongside the tree, took off his hat, then stretched out. Exhausted, his eyes glazed over.

Dear Reader!

If you enjoyed this book, please check out my website, dathanbelanger-author.com, to learn about current and ensuing books.

While you're there, please join my mailing list. And don't forget to give me and my books a shout-out on your social media platforms.

—Dathan

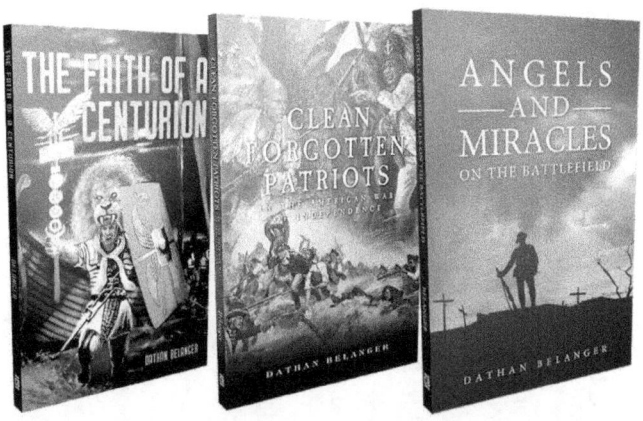